"My man never saw the faces of his attackers," Dex said. "He wouldn't be able to identify them ... the five who attacked him were all wearing hoods."

Mr. Barr went suddenly pale and for a moment Dex thought he was having palpitations.

"Sir?" Dex leaped from his chair and raced around the table to crouch by the old man's side. "Sir? Are you all right?"

"I am ... thank you, Dexter. Your mention of them ... I'm afraid it startled me. They are ... evil. That is the only way to describe them. They are Satan's spawn, Dexter, and my advice to you is for you to take your man and leave. Do not even consider opposing them. I'd not like to see Charles Yancey's son become their next victim. I want you to leave here just as quickly as you are able."

"You advice is well intentioned. I know that. But will you tell me what you can of these men?"

"All I know of them, Dexter, is the name they collectively call themselves. They are the Knights of the Klu Klux Klan, Dexter, and they are as evil as their Satanic master ..."

DON'T MISS THESE
ALL-ACTION WESTERN SERIES
FROM THE BERKLEY PUBLISHING GROUP

THE GUNSMITH by J. R. Roberts
Clint Adams was a legend among lawmen, outlaws, and ladies.
They called him . . . the Gunsmith.

LONGARM by Tabor Evans
The popular long-running series about U.S. Deputy Marshal
Long—his life, his loves, his fight for justice.

SLOCUM by Jake Logan
Today's longest-running action Western. John Slocum rides
a deadly trail of hot blood and cold steel.

BUSHWHACKERS by B. J. Lanagan
An action-packed series by the creators of Longarm! The
rousing adventures of the most brutal gang of cutthroats
ever assembled—Quantrill's Raiders.

DIAMONDBACK
RAKING IN REVENGE

◆ ◆ ◆

Guy Brewer

JOVE BOOKS, NEW YORK

If you purchased this book without a cover, you should be aware that this book is stolen property. It was reported as "unsold and destroyed" to the publisher and neither the author nor the publisher has received any payment for this "stripped book."

This is a work of fiction. Names, characters, places, and incidents are either the product of the author's imagination or are used fictitiously, and any resemblance to actual persons, living or dead, business establishments, events, or locales is entirely coincidental.

DIAMONDBACK: RAKING IN REVENGE

A Jove Book / published by arrangement with
the author

PRINTING HISTORY
Jove edition / February 2000

All rights reserved.
Copyright © 2000 by Penguin Putnam Inc.
This book may not be reproduced in whole or in part,
by mimeograph or any other means, without permission.
For information address: The Berkley Publishing Group,
a division of Penguin Putnam Inc.,
375 Hudson Street, New York, New York 10014.

The Penguin Putnam Inc. World Wide Web site address is
http://www.penguinputnam.com

ISBN: 0-515-12753-1

A JOVE BOOK®
Jove Books are published by The Berkley Publishing Group,
a division of Penguin Putnam Inc.,
375 Hudson Street, New York, New York 10014.
JOVE and the "J" design
are trademarks belonging to Penguin Putnam Inc.

PRINTED IN THE UNITED STATES OF AMERICA

10 9 8 7 6 5 4 3 2 1

◆ 1 ◆

If all the women in Texas were like this one, he'd never leave. Or want to.

Her name was Jane, but she damn sure wasn't plain. She was, in a word, gorgeous.

She had hair like spun gold and tits so magnificent they deserved names. He'd told her so, actually. And her response had been . . . well, "amazing" came to mind.

He'd only done it for a lark, and if the truth be known there was the added factor of half a dozen excellent brandies taken on an otherwise empty stomach.

They had been in attendance at a gala hosted by a gentleman named Barr, an old friend of Dexter's father. The music was poor and the dance floor crowded, and Dex had taken his latest brandy outside into the garden in search of cool air untainted by cigar smoke.

He'd found rather more than that.

He rounded a turn in the brick path to discover Jane—he hadn't known her by name at the time of course—seated alone on a stone bench with a silver cup of syrupy sweet fruit punch at her side.

"You're handsome," she said when she saw him. "What's your name?"

Dex was flattered, if a trifle taken aback. And in truth he never did fully understand why the ladies often viewed him with favor. Not that he was complaining, mind. But it did seem mildly curious to him.

After all, he was quite ordinary enough in his own estimation. He stood slightly under six feet in height and was not overly muscular. Rather he had a lean and wiry frame, dark blond hair, and Burnside whiskers along the shelf of a strong jawline. He had brown eyes and was dressed well if not grandly in tight-fitting light gray trousers, a darker charcoal swallowtail coat, pearl gray planters hat, and highly polished black stovepipe boots.

When the buxom golden girl made her bold inquiry Dex planted himself on the bench beside her without waiting for an invitation. "Dexter Lee Yancey," he said with a tip of his hat. And then on wicked impulse looked downward into the gaping décolletage at the front of her gown and asked, "And what are their names?"

The blonde girl seemed stunned by the question. But only for a moment. She threw back her pretty head and roared out her laughter. "A real man!" she exclaimed. "At last."

"In short supply around here, are they?"

"There don't seem to be any willing to risk my daddy's wrath by courting me," she said.

"In case he asks," Dex said, "you can tell your daddy that I've no intention of courting you."

She made a pout. The expression was not one Dex normally liked, but he had to admit that it did some rather interesting things to her mouth. For the second time he gave rein to his impulses. He leaned forward and tasted of that mouth. The girl's lips were as soft and mobile as they were attractive, and he could not help noticing that not only did she refrain from pulling away from him, she began to return the kiss.

After a few moments she made a small, furry sound somewhere deep in her throat, and he felt the quick, flickering probe of her tongue.

Five or six minutes later, having ascertained that her breasts were nicely firm for jugs of such impressive size, Dex broke off the embrace and said, "You never did get around to telling me your name yet."

"Do you really care?" she countered.

"It would be nice to know what I should call you when we wake up tomorrow."

"You're a bold son of a bitch, aren't you?"

He shrugged. "If you don't mind it, I'm perfectly willing to live with a simple 'hey you'."

The girl laughed again and reached for the brandy that he somehow still held. "Give me some of that. Those high-collar bastards inside would be scandalized if I asked for one of my own."

Dex relinquished his brandy, and the girl tossed it down in a gulp. She winced, shuddered, then smiled hugely. "I needed that."

"I'd go get you more but people might wonder why the buttons of my fly precede me by half a yard."

"Braggart," she said. Then reached down and felt of him. Her eyes went wide. "But only by a little. Damn!"

That, he conceded, was another reason why some of the ladies proved fond of him.

"I think I'll call you Brassy," he said, "because you are as bold as."

"At least it is more interesting than the truth. My name, if you must know, is Jane. Plain, ugly, simple Jane. Not Jane Ann. Not Jane Louise. Not Jane Darling. Just . . . Jane."

"Jane," he said slowly, as if tasting it. "But not plain and certainly not ugly."

"I meant the name, not me, stupid."

"I was trying to be gallant."

"Thank you for explaining that." She was laughing silently to herself, obviously having a good time. He had to wonder if Jane was all talk.

So he asked, "You scrub up pretty nice, but are you a good fuck, Plain Jane?"

"Better than you've ever had," she snapped.

"Care to prove that?"

"That sounds like a challenge to me," she said.

"Ayuh, so it is. Your claim is that you'll be the best I've ever known. Fine. I'm willing to make the same boast with you."

"Who do we ask to referee this event?" she asked.

"That could be a problem, of course. Unless you are more wanton than good sense would allow. How about we settle for self-evaluation on the honor system."

"But can I trust you?"

"Every bit as much as I can trust you," he said.

"In that event, Mr. Yancey, I suggest we repair to the carriage house."

• 2 •

"Ouch, dammit!"

"Did I hurt you?"

She grabbed him. "No, don't take it out, you idiot. It feels good there."

"But you said—"

"You didn't hurt me. It's my ankle. I scraped it on the flower vase thing there. I think I cut myself. I think I'm bleeding."

Dex looked. It was dark inside the carriage house, but his eyes had adjusted and he could see well enough to tell that Jane was not bleeding and probably wasn't even scratched. "You're all right."

"You're sure?"

"Positive."

"Then stop talking and pay attention to your driving," she demanded.

Dex put his attention back where it belonged and resumed stroking slowly in and out. The feelings were really quite extraordinary, probably having to do with the angle involved and the extreme amount of penetration that was made possible.

They were in the back of a rather nice brougham that Jane had selected from among the several buggies, carriages, and carts that were kept in the Barr carriage house. The four-passenger vehicle with its driving box separate from the closed passenger compartment had soft leather upholstery that served nicely as a temporary trysting place.

Jane had no inhibitions about stripping completely naked, the better to enjoy the experience, and demanded that Dex too remove every vestige of clothing. Now she had one very shapely leg braced on the floor while the other was propped high on the back of the brougham seat. The position left her spread very wide open for him, with her hips tilted at an angle that allowed him an unusual degree of depth and movement atop the girl's body.

Dex had been experimenting with the possibilities of motion when Jane interrupted with her complaints about blood and gore.

"There," she said when he returned to the not particularly arduous task at hand. "That's nice." He agreed. "Yes, like that. Deeper now. Slowly. And . . . yesss!" Her hips arched upward to meet him in a wildly passionate thrust of her own, and he could feel her limbs tremble and quiver as shuddering jolts of pleasure ran through her like waves on a seashore. Jane flailed her legs about and then clamped them tight around him.

Her breathing quickened and became ragged, and after a moment she went utterly limp beneath him. He was not sure but believed that the girl might actually have passed out for a few moments there although she recovered quickly enough.

"That was wonderful," she said. "Thank you."

"My pleasure, ma'am." He began to stroke into her again.

Jane placed a hand on his slightly sweaty chest and pushed. "I'm done now," she said.

"So I gathered," he said. "It felt like it was good for you."

"It was, but I won't make it again. You can stop now."

"I haven't come yet."

"Well, I have. So get off me. You're heavy. Your leg is hurting me, and I want a drink."

"I told you, I haven't come yet."

"You can finish with your hand. Now let me up."

Dex raised an eyebrow. He did not, however, raise his hips. His cock remained socketed warm and wet and deep inside the blonde beauty's body.

"I said—"

He thrust forward. Hard. And again.

"Don't. Damn you—" She pushed at him with both hands and tried to squirm out from underneath him.

Dexter laughed and let the girl's struggles serve to increase the motion and the feeling. He'd been near to the bursting point himself a minute or so earlier and it took little now to send him spilling over the edge and into Jane.

"Damn you," she complained. "What if you've gone and made me pregnant?"

"Afterward is not the time to be thinking about something like that," he said. It seemed a reasonable enough statement to him. Apparently Jane did not agree. She balled up a fist and punched him in the belly.

"Hey. That hurts."

"Serves you right," she said. "I never said you could make me pregnant."

"No, and I probably haven't. I sort of assumed you knew how to avoid that or you wouldn't be so free to drop your knickers."

"Are you saying I am loose, sir?"

Dex looked at her, lying with her legs sprawled about as far apart as it was possible to spread them, still sweaty and trembling from her own amorous exertions, naked, with a complete stranger's dick still inside her pussy . . . and now she wanted him to think of her as chaste and demure?

He couldn't help himself.

Her question was simply too ludicrous to believe.

He burst out laughing.

That was, he determined, the wrong damn thing to do.

◆ 3 ◆

"**Y**ou look like hell," Dex's best friend, James, greeted him. "I hope you at least got some licks in of your own."

Dex scowled but didn't answer.

"You're back early too. Party turn into a brawl, did it?" James laughed. "I didn't think you high class white boys knew how to have fun like that." James himself happened to be of a chocolate hue. Once upon a time he'd been Dexter's playtoy, a slave on the Yancey plantation in Louisiana. Circumstance—and a bit of warfare—had altered that status. What remained despite law and custom was a deep and genuine friendship, although it was a relationship the two kept to themselves. There were few people, white or black, who would be willing to accept simple friendship. For the most part when in public James posed as Dex's servant and employee.

"You aren't saying much, I notice," James teased. "The other guy get the best of you, did he?"

Dex shrugged.

"Come to think of it . . . is that a scratch I see on the side of your neck there?"

Dex was undressing in preparation for bed, and as he pulled his shirt off James began to laugh all the louder.

"When I'm with them," James said, "they sometimes scratch my back or my shoulders. Occasionally some little ol' gal will get really rambunctious and rake her nails on my butt so that it stings. But Dexter, Dexter, Dexter." He shook his head in mock sadness. "Those are most definitely scratch marks on your chest. Do you mean to tell me that it was some woman who marked you up like that? Lordy, Lordy. Just think. In a fistfight and you couldn't even hit back. Dexter, Dexter? Aren't you talking to me any more? Are you there, Dexter? It *was* a woman, wasn't it."

"Not that it's any of your business, but . . . yes."

"Well let this be a lesson to you. It isn't nice to go around getting fresh with strangers. What'd you do, pinch her butt or something?"

"Something," Dex said. "We'll just let it go at that."

James laughed again, then stood and stretched. Except for his color he actually looked a great deal like Dexter, both of them having lean and athletic builds. James was slightly the taller of the two and was the younger by almost a year.

As children they had been well matched, James constantly at Dexter's side, attending school as the white boy's servant—listening and learning throughout each of the lessons that were intended for Dex—acting as his partner or opponent as required when it came to riding, fencing, wrestling, running, shooting or whatever other endeavors were deemed appropriate for a young Southern gentleman of means.

"Come here, dammit," James said.

"Now what?"

"Oh, don't act so surly. I'm not the one that scratched you. And I do take note of the fact that you had your shirt off when it happened, so the evening probably wasn't a total loss." James' grin flashed. "Well, not up to that point anyway."

"So what d'you want now?" Dex demanded.

"I have some of that balm my mama packed for me. It will take the sting out of those scratches and help them heal over. A cat or a woman either one, Dex, you'd best be careful of their scratches for you never know where those claws have been."

Dexter grumbled some. But he also allowed James to rummage through his saddlebags and find the tiny jar of foul-smelling ointment to smear on the open wounds. Dex did, after all, know good advice when he heard it. And at this point he was quite willing to believe that Miss Jane—he never had gotten her last name, come to think of it—was poison on the hoof.

• 4 •

"So," James asked as he finished tying his shoe laces in preparation to face the morning, "what do you have planned today?"

"I promised Mr. Barr that I'd have lunch with him. You?"

James shook his head. "Nothing. To tell you the truth I was hoping we could move along today."

"Bored with Wharburton already, are you?" They had been there—Dex had to think back for a moment—this was their fourth day in town.

"In a word . . . yes," James told him. "Unlike some folks that I might name, I don't have any old family friends here. And in case you don't already know it, let me tell you something else. Us dinges aren't exactly welcomed with open arms by the good townsfolk. In fact, there aren't a whole hell of a lot of black faces on display."

"I hadn't noticed."

"Well I damn sure have," James said firmly.

"I grant that you have a somewhat . . . shall we say . . . different perspective on the subject."

"Dammit, Dexter, the only friendly face I've seen since we got here is yours."

"I could scowl at you," Dex suggested. "Make your day complete."

"I'm serious, Dexter. I'd like to move down the road again just as quick as we can, if it's all the same to you."

"All right. There isn't anything chaining me here either. But I did make that promise to the old man. How about if I keep my word, then tomorrow morning we can saddle up and . . . I don't know . . . head for Austin?"

"Austin sounds better than here." James frowned. "Far as I can see, white boy, almost anyplace sounds better to me than here."

"We'll leave tomorrow morning then."

James' mood brightened. "I was afraid you're so enamored of that girl who beat you up last night that you wouldn't want to leave."

It was Dex's turn to frown. "If I never see her again, and I mean not in this lifetime or the next, it will be quite soon enough to suit me."

"She must be a real pistol."

"A pisser is more like it."

"Yeah, well, come tomorrow morning you won't have to ever think about her again," James suggested.

"That sounds just fine to me. Say, though. Have you seen my socks? I thought I put them right over here. Now they're gone."

James, shaking his head sadly, plucked the errant stockings from the floor beneath the hotel room wardrobe and tossed them into Dexter's lap. "I sweah," he said, his voice becoming syrupy, "why couldn't I o' drawn me a smaht man fo' my old massuh?"

· 5 ·

"Mr. Yancey. So nice to see you, sir."

Dexter handed his hat and cane to the housekeeper, a red-cheeked little fat Irishwoman whose name he thought was Mrs. Collum. He did not trust that memory quite far enough to address her by name however. "Thank you. Is Mr. Barr in?"

Dex thought the lady looked to be a mite puzzled. "Was he expecting you, Mr. Yancey?"

"We were to have lunch together."

"Goodness. He didn't mention anything about it to me."

It was Dex's turn to be puzzled. "Last night he said—"

"Please forgive him, Mr. Yancey. He may well have forgotten the invitation. Perhaps I'm speaking out of turn, but the truth is that he has been . . . terribly distracted lately."

"I certainly don't want to bother him. If he's forgotten I can just go on back to the hotel, and—"

"No, please don't do that. Your visit will be good for him, I'm sure. I believe he's in the garden. Can you find your way there?"

"Of course."

Mrs. Collum smiled. "Good, because I need to hurry the cook along with lunch. I hope you don't require anything fancy."

"The pleasure will be in the company. Potluck will do nicely for me, thank you."

She curtsied and scurried away toward the back of the huge house, leaving Dexter to make his way through the hall where there had been so much dancing and gaiety last night—it looked dreary and forlorn today with the party trappings not yet removed and no merrymakers in sight—and out into the garden.

Dex could not help remembering that his memories of that garden were not altogether unpleasant. Nor completely enjoyable either, it was true. Miss Jane was quite the beauty. Quite the wanton. Quite also the pain in the ass.

Still, it wasn't either Jane or the handsomely tended garden that brought him here. He stepped out along the path in search of the old gentleman who once had been a friend, if not a close companion, of Dexter's father.

Dexter rounded a turn in the path and came in sight of the bench where last night he'd first seen the golden-haired vixen with those magnificent tits. And, he recalled quite painfully well, with a temper proportionate in abundance to her mammaries.

Edgar Barr was standing beside that same bench this forenoon, his back toward Dexter.

The old man held a cocked pistol pressed tight against his right temple. His posture was rigid. Uncompromising. He took in a long, deep breath, his shoulders rising slightly as he did so.

Then Dex could see his knuckles whiten as his grip grew tight on the butt of the big, old-fashioned horse pistol.

♦ 6 ♦

"No!"

Dex lunged forward, throwing himself at Barr, his hand sweeping up to batter the pistol barrel aside.

Either Barr was already squeezing the trigger or Dex's sudden motion caused the pistol to fire. A spear of bright yellow flame erupted from the flared muzzle, and there was a dull, booming report more like that of a shotgun than the crack of a pistol. But then the antique muzzle-loading horse pistol had a bore the size of a shotgun.

Barr, startled, spun around. His silver hair was disheveled and there was a haunted look in his eyes. "You shouldn't . . . oh God, young man, you should not have interfered. You should have let me . . . go away. Please. Leave." Barr's shoulders were trembling, and Dex thought he looked close to tears.

Well, that seemed reasonable enough. A man did not undertake to blow his own brains out if his mood were cheery and fine.

"Sir. Please." Dex reached out and gently extracted the pistol from Barr's unresisting hand. The damn thing must have weighed four pounds or more. Certainly it would be as useful as a club than as a firearm. Perhaps more so because having been discharged it would require a tedious reloading process before it could fire again.

"You don't know . . . you shouldn't have—" Barr gained some small measure of control over himself. His posture straightened as he came to his full height, and he looked Dex in the eye for the first time. "You will have to excuse me, young man." Barr smoothed his hair down with both hands and looked much the better for it. "May I have my weapon back if you please?"

Dexter bowed. "As you wish, sir." He handed the old gun back. It was, after all, empty and no threat to anyone now.

Barr's hand, Dex noticed, was steady when he took the pistol. The old man was a gentleman, no doubt about it. In the midst of all this he retained his dignity and his self control.

"Why are you here, young Yancey? I . . . oh, my. I do remember now. I asked you to lunch today, didn't I?"

"You did, sir." Dex smiled. "And I fully intend to hold you to that invitation."

"I neglected to tell the cook. You will forgive me, I hope?"

"Of course, sir. As to the cook, your housekeeper . . . Mrs. Collum, is it?"

Barr nodded. "You've a good memory."

"Yes, sir. Good enough to recall my father's fondness for you. Anyway, Mrs. Collum is taking care of our luncheon preparations. I shouldn't want to disappoint her now."

Barr gave Dex a level, speculative look, no doubt seeking the things that were unsaid as well as those that were stated. After a moment he dropped his gaze and glanced down to the pistol in his hand. "Remind me to clean this after lunch, will you?"

"Yes, sir. My father always taught me, though, that it's best to keep a pistol clean but unloaded when it's in storage. The powder can be corrosive on the metal within."

"Aye, and there are things within a man that can corrode his mettle, too. Is that what you're telling me, boy?"

"I would not presume to advise you, sir. Not without invitation."

"You've been invited to lunch."

"Yes, sir."

"Perhaps . . . perhaps we will chat after. While I clean the pistol, eh?"

Dex smiled. "I would like that, sir."

"Hmmph, yes, well, we shall see what we shall see."

"Yes, sir. As you wish, Mr. Barr. As you wish."

• 7 •

The old man exhibited much more interest in a postprandial brandy than he had in his lunch. He'd eaten hardly a morsel. But then, Dex reflected, so close a brush with death seemed an apt enough cause for losing one's appetite. Barr had been no more than a quarter ounce of pressure and half a heartbeat of time away from coming face-to-face—what little might have been left of it—with the grim reaper.

"This is excellent brandy, sir. Thank you." It wasn't what he was really thinking, of course.

"It's French, you know," Barr said proudly.

"Yes, sir." As a Louisianan, Dex knew he was expected to revere France and all things French. As a northern Louisianan, however, he did not. He said nothing about that at the moment, however. And the brandy really was quite good, regardless of where it came from.

"I suppose," Barr added in a slow, halting voice, "you would like an explanation about . . . recent events."

"You owe me no explanations, sir. But I stand willing to serve you in any way that I can. I know my father would have. I will do no less, Mr. Barr."

Barr sighed and gazed blindly toward a horizon that lay somewhere far beyond the boundaries of this paneled and handsome study. After a moment, his eyes still unfocused, he said, "Your father was a fine man, Dexter. A good friend. I was sorry to hear of his passing."

"Thank you, sir." Dex doubted that Barr heard him.

The old man sighed. "It was good when Charles and I were young. Things were different then. Better."

"Yes, sir."

"Government was better then, you know. There wasn't all this interference with . . . things. A man was allowed to stand or to fall on his own strengths and merit."

"Yes, sir."

"There was no thuggery either. I came here early, you know. Cut the timber. Put plow to soil that never was turned until the day I claimed it from the forest and the field." He smiled and turned his head, seemed actually to see Dex sitting there again. "Did you know that the first seed I planted came from your father's fields? Your granddaddy's they would have been then, of course. But it was your father who helped me get my start. Helped me choose my seed. Went with me to the auctions when I bought my labor. Even made me the loan of some of his own hands to ensure that I could make a crop that first season. Did you know that?"

"No, sir, I didn't."

"It is true, Dexter. I owe a great debt to your father." Barr smiled just a little. "And to your granddaddy, too, of course, although he never knew that." The old gentleman managed a sharp little bark of laughter. "He never knew a thing about that, no sir he did not. Six field hands, a wench, and the use of a big, fine, strapping stud nigger for that whole first season, and your granddaddy never knew the first thing about it. That was your father's doing. But then we'd been close friends at school. You did know that, did you not?"

"Yes, sir. He certainly talked about that often."

"Emory College, all the way over to Oxford, Georgia. Have you ever seen it?"

"I matriculated there too, sir."

"Did you indeed, son? I didn't know that." Barr showed some genuine interest for the first time, and for the next hour or more talked quite gaily about the years he and a young Charles Yancey spent at the fine little school.

Dex did not mind listening to the old man's memories. The places were familiar if not the names. And, perhaps not so oddly, it gave him a glimpse into his own father's youth, a time and indeed a person Dex had never before really considered. Hearing of a young Charles Yancey's escapades gave Dexter pause. His father's boyhood shenanigans brought to life a person Dex himself never knew, and he was genuinely sorry when old Mr. Barr's well of reminiscence ran dry.

Eventually though the elderly gentleman lapsed into silence, his thoughts once more wandering to places where Dexter could not, should not follow.

"It is all going now, you know," he said in a very sad, small voice. "All going."

"Sir?"

Barr shivered, blinked, and sat stiffly upright in a faded old wingback chair. "Nothing. It doesn't matter."

"Sir, I do want you to know that . . . well . . . if there is anything I can do—"

Barr smiled. "You've done much already," he said. "I've enjoyed this chance to talk about what it was like those long years back."

"Yes, sir. I have enjoyed this, too."

"You sound as if you mean that, Dexter."

"Good, sir, because I do."

"Fine. And as for . . . what happened in the garden—"

"You needn't talk about that, sir. But I hope you won't . . . that is—"

"I know what you mean, son, and I thank you for your concern. I'll make you no promises about the future though. I'll give no guarantees that I cannot keep, sir."

"I would not expect less from a gentleman like you, Mr. Barr."

The old man cleared his throat and shifted in his chair but looked pleased nonetheless.

"Would you make me a small promise, sir?" Dex asked. "One that you can keep?"

"Yes, of course. I certainly owe you that much, if only for the pleasure of your company today."

"Would you promise me you'll make no, shall we say, irrevocable decisions? Not for the next, oh, two or three months? I think this is something you should give very serious thought to, sir. Please."

"Surely you know that I have already thought upon my situation at great length."

"Yes, sir, I am sure you have. But please. What harm can another few months make?"

"Three months? I don't think—"

"Two then. Would you promise me another two months of contemplation? That isn't too much to ask surely."

"Two months?" Barr looked away for a moment, then nodded. "All right. Two months." He smiled again. "I owe your father that much consideration, Dexter. And now you as well. Two months it is."

"Thank you, sir. And perhaps in that time things will, well, improve?"

Barr's answering bark was not laughter this time but hopeless, helpless derision of such an idea. "Dexter, son, there are some things that time will not heal nor procrastination improve. I expect no changes. But to look upon the brighter side of things, son, I can no longer be disappointed, can I?"

"So you see, sir? There is a bright side, right?"

"If I were your age, Dexter, I might see it that way, too. But I am too old a man and too set in my ways to change now. Perhaps, after the war, I could have started over then. I was young enough then. I could have begun something new. But not now. Not at this late stage in life."

"Sir, you did promise—"

"And I shall hold to my word, Dexter. Have no doubt of that."

"No, sir, I have none."

"Would you care for another brandy, son?"

"Thank you, sir, but I'll be going now. I plan to leave in the morning and want to make sure my servant has our things packed and ready."

Barr stood and offered his hand. "Your company has been a rare and special pleasure, Dexter. Thank you for having this time with me."

"I doubt that I'll see you again, Mr. Barr, but you will remain in my thoughts and you will continue to have my finest and fullest wishes." Dex shook the old man's hand and went off to retrieve his hat and cane from Mrs. Collum.

· 8 ·

Dex worried about the old man. A little, anyway. It wasn't like he knew Mr. Barr well. Still, he hoped he'd done the right thing back there. Stopping him from shooting himself . . . of course it was right to do that. It was the conversation afterward in which Dex felt he probably hadn't done enough.

He should have had words of encouragement. Some magic phrasing that would lift Mr. Barr from his malaise and make him want to go on.

Well dammit, Dex didn't know any such words or phrases. He had no easy solutions for problems that were completely unclear to him.

A month. He'd gotten Mr. Barr to pause and consider, and the old man had at least a month in which to do that.

Dex's worry now was to wonder if that was time enough for Mr. Barr's problems to be resolved . . . or if a month from now, his promise having been met, the gentleman would finish what he'd tried to start today and splatter his brains over half the garden.

Not, thank goodness, that Dexter would ever know the outcome. It would be better, he supposed, to venture on with the assumption that sometime in the weeks to come Mr. Barr would reach accommodation with whatever fears and worries haunted him and that in a month's time the old gentleman would have forgotten this incident entirely or at the very least would have put it behind him.

Dex himself was more than anxious to put Mr. Barr and his worries behind. Whatever his problems were, he hadn't chosen to speak of them and so Dexter could ride on with a clear conscience. He'd done what he could to help his father's old friend and college roommate, and that was the end of it.

Dex reached the hotel and took the steps two at a time onto the broad veranda that ran across the front of the building. "Good afternoon, Anderson," Dex said to the hotel clerk as he entered. "Is my servant upstairs?"

Eager as James was to leave Wharburton, Dex figured by now their saddlebags would be packed and the horses already groomed in readiness for an early morning departure.

"No, sir. I saw him leave this morning, but he hasn't come back yet."

Dex shrugged. It didn't matter. It was still hours short of suppertime, and there was no telling where James had gotten to. In public the two of them were quite comfortably accustomed to their lifelong practice of pretending still that James was a servant, but in truth it never would have occurred to Dexter to order James around. James was as free to go and to do as Dex himself was.

"I'll be leaving tomorrow," Dex told Anderson. "It probably wouldn't hurt to take care of my bill now, just in case I wake early and decide to start off in the cool of the morning."

"As you wish, sir."

Anderson—Dex never had quite decided if that was the man's first name or last—withdrew a ledger from a drawer beneath the counter and spent an amazingly long time trying to add the few figures necessary to arrive at a final billing amount. A nice man, no doubt, but not overwhelmed with an excess of intelligence, Dex concluded.

"Will you be charging dinner for yourself and the nigger tonight, sir?"

"No, I'll pay cash at the table if I eat here."

Anderson went back to his calculations, the tip of his tongue showing wet and pink in the corner of his mouth as he concentrated. "Ah. Yes. Here you go, sir."

Anderson spun his book around and with it the bit of paper he'd been figuring on.

The amount displayed was a round two dollars more than it should have been.

Maybe Anderson wasn't so dumb as he made himself out to be, Dex considered without rancor.

He pointed to the error, received the obligatory apology, and paid the amended and now correct amount.

Anderson at least had the good grace to hide his disappointment that he would not be able to pocket a surplus.

"Thank you for staying with us, Mr. Yancey. You come back any time now, hear?"

Dex nodded and went upstairs to a room that looked exactly as it had when he left to join Mr. Barr.

Since James hadn't gotten to it, Dex busied himself by packing for both of them. With James so anxious to put Wharburton behind them, Dex thought, they just might make an early start of it come morning. After all, they could always stop at virtually any farmstead along the way and be sure of finding a meal. And probably at better price and quality than the hotel would provide.

· 9 ·

James had said there were few blacks in Wharburton but he must have found at least one other to spend some time with and probably a young and pretty female at that, Dex guessed as suppertime approached with no sign of James. If the girl were pretty enough James might not be so anxious to move on, he considered.

Not that it really made all that much difference. They were on no schedule, had no meetings to attend nor coaches to catch. They were young, free, and footloose and best of all they had a satisfyingly large lump of currency—most of them high denomination bills, thank you—inside the money belt that James wore.

The two of them shared the wealth, such as it was, each using whatever he needed or wished from a mutually held total, but James kept the cash on his person under the theory that a robber would certainly shake down Dexter but would be unlikely to suspect a simple Negro servant of having money on him. And James could play the mush-mouthed simpleton to good effect if or when he wished. Dex kept only enough in his pockets to meet their daily needs and, hopefully, to allay suspicion in the unlikely event that they encountered a highwayman somewhere in their travels.

Dex gave up waiting for James as the sun was receding behind a stand of live oak behind the hotel building. James could fend for himself, dammit. And lunch was some hours past. Dex was getting hungry.

He went downstairs to dinner and enjoyed a solid if uninspired meal, then decided he would see to the horses and treat himself to a few drinks before a planned early retirement for the evening. He wanted to get a good night's sleep before striking out tomorrow.

Dex paid cash for his supper, then ambled outside. He nodded a good evening to three hotel guests who were relaxing in rocking chairs on the veranda and passed a few idle pleasantries with them before strolling through soft evening air to the public stable where the horses were boarded, the Wharburton hotel not having accommodation for travelers' stock.

"Good evening," Dex said to the lean old fellow who tended the place. "Everything all right?"

"Just fine, mister."

"I'll be wanting my horses along about dawn tomorrow. Feed them early if you would, please. Hay free choice overnight and, say, three quarters of grain before first light. Oats and bran only, though. No corn. I don't want them fed too hot."

"Your nigger already told me 'bout the same except he said it'd be all right if I gave some barley in the grain mix. That be all right with you, mister?"

"Just fine. You said my man already told you that?"

"It's what I said, yes. Shouldn't he've done that?"

"No, it's fine. I just . . . when did he tell you this?"

"I dunno. Past lunch sometime. Said you told him to tell me."

"That's right," Dex fibbed. "I forgot." He grinned. "He hasn't come back to the hotel since, though. Must've found a little old gal to slow him down."

The liveryman snorted. "Not in this town, mister. No wenches around here. No niggers at all. We don't allow 'em."

Dex frowned. Not about the law in Wharburton. He'd come across more than one community where signs were posted prohibiting the presence of Negroes beyond sundown, and regardless of his personal opinion about such things he believed a town was entirely within its rights to set out whatever rules its citizenry wished.

That didn't bother him at all.

But if James wasn't off dallying with some dark-skinned maiden . . . then just where the hell was he?

· 10 ·

Seeing dawn arrive before James did was not something that would normally be worrisome. This time it was. And all the more so as time continued to pass.

At eight Dex went downstairs to have breakfast. They'd intended to get an early start and then find a place along the way to breakfast, but that wasn't working out and by eight Dex was hungry. Until he was seated in the dining room actually contemplating the menu. The thought of food only soured a stomach that was already upset with worry. He pushed away from the table without having so much as a cup of coffee and walked down to the livery barn.

The horses were there but James was not.

"No," the liveryman said in response to Dexter's query. "Haven't seen anything of your nigger since yesterday that I already told you about." The man fingered his chin and acted like he intended to speak but did not.

"What is it?" Dex asked.

"Nothin'."

"You were going to say something just then. Tell me. Please."

"It's just . . . prob'ly nothing, that's what it is, mister. An' damn sure it's none o' my affair."

"Tell me. I won't let on where I heard it if that's what is worrying you."

"It's just . . . like I said, it prob'ly has nothin' at all to do with you an' sure as shooting has nothing to do with me. But I heard there was a nigger killed yesterday. Not so many of those around town these days, you know. That's why I was thinking it might've been your nigger."

Dex felt a hard, chill knot develop in his gut. "Killed?" he repeated.

"That's what I heard."

"Who would know about it, man? Where can I find him?"

"Don't know as there's anything *to* find, mind you—"

"Dammit, man, quit being so shit-picky with your words and tell me," Dex snapped, his patience—what little of it he possessed to begin with—worn mighty thin by now.

"You might could ask the sherf."

"The sheriff?"

"His deputy actually. Sherf himself stays over to the county seat. This end of the county is taken care of by Deputy Barney Garrison. Has an office right smack behind the town building. You go a block that way, mister, and turn to your right, then—"

The livery man was not finished with his rambling dissertation when Dex wheeled and hurried off in the direction the man indicated.

James dead? That seemed . . . No. Dammit no. He would *not* believe it.

Not unless . . .

Dex's long stride lengthened into a trot and then into an all-out run.

He had to know. Whatever the truth, he had to know.

• 11 •

Deputy Barney Garrison was a large man, meaty and strong and self-assured. He stood at least six feet two and was piled wide as well as high. In his late forties or thereabouts, very little of his heft was fat.

There was something about him, in his eyes and demeanor alike, that suggested he could be one mean son of a bitch if the mood took him. And he looked like a man who often indulged in exactly that sort of mood.

At the moment, however, he was indifferent. He obviously recognized that Dex was not a local and therefore was likely to be of little interest or importance. "What can I do for you, mister?" he asked without any particular show of haste or alarm when Dex burst into his tiny office.

"I heard . . . that is to say . . . my manservant is missing. Since yesterday. I heard there was a Negro killed yesterday. And I thought—"

"Manservant, eh?" Dex was acutely aware of Garrison's scrutiny as the deputy looked him over, obviously judging this distraught visitor's social standing and probable wealth.

"He's a black man, like I said. His name is James. He was my slave once; now he is my servant." That part was very much deliberate albeit not something Dex normally would have so readily disclosed. He wanted Garrison to have no doubt about what class the Yanceys came from, and here in Texas a man of Barney Garrison's age was almost certain to have a virtually inbred measure of respect and admiration for a gentleman whose people were—or rather had been—slaveholders.

"James, eh? Didn't know his name of course."

"You . . . is it true? Is he really dead?"

Garrison shrugged. "Not yet. Son of a bitch nigger's slow to die. You know what I mean? Or anyhow he wasn't dead yet the last time I looked. Damn shame too. Sam Yonanecker does the burying for the county, and he's hoping the nig croaks before close of business today or the county clerk won't pay Sam for the burying until next month's budget." Garrison paused to think for a moment, then brightened considerably. "Come to think of it, mister, could be that you'd be willing to go the price of the burying. County pays two dollars. You should ought to know that. Sam will ask you more, but he'll do it for the usual two dollars. Course you could just walk away now and the county will pay. But it'd be the right and Christian thing was you to pay for the burying seeing as it's your nigger that's dying."

"He isn't dead yet though?" Dex asked.

Garrison shrugged again. "Damn if I know, mister. I looked in on him this morning when I come over from the house. Haven't checked on him since. Can't really say for sure if he's dead yet or ain't."

"Where?"

Garrison hooked a thumb over his shoulder, aiming it in the general vicinity of the back wall of his office. "Got a shed out back. We put him in there to finish his dying."

"The doctor," Dex said. "What did the doctor say?"

Garrison only shrugged again. The big man did not bother speaking.

Dex gave up the useless questioning. He turned and bolted from the deputy's office, sprinting around behind the building to find, to comfort, if nothing else to say good-bye to his oldest and dearest friend.

· 12 ·

They hadn't even laid him out decently. Someone—the sons of bitches should hope he never found out who—just carried him inside the shed and dumped him there. And that was likely an effort to get him out of sight rather than from any notion of comfort or kindness. Jesus! Dex thought.

James lay in a crumpled heap beside the dry and ancient bars of what once had been a horse stall. Now it was filled with cast-off junk and smelled of must and mold and dust.

Dex knelt beside his friend, brought close to tears by the horrible things that had been done to him.

James was barely recognizable from the beating he'd taken. His head was distorted with swelling and blackened with dried blood. His eyes were closed, swollen shut, and covered with yellowish pus.

Flies crawled unmolested in and out of the dark, empty cavity of James' mouth. His right arm lay bent at a sickeningly impossible angle, and there was no lift or fall of breath visible in his bare chest. The remnants of what had been his clothing hung in a tangle beneath his still form.

James had, Dex concluded, passed on. Mercifully so, he supposed. But Lord, it was hard to believe that. A mere cessation of pain is hardly fair value in exchange for a life relinquished.

Dex bowed his head and squeezed his eyes tight shut and tried to bring prayerful words to mind. His eyes burned and moisture trickled down across his cheeks, but neither prayer nor comfort came from his efforts.

God seemed very far away at this moment.

Dex opened his eyes and rubbed the back of his wrist over them.

James. Whatever was Dex ever going to tell James' mother? A lie probably. A lie that might be less painful to her than this mean and miserable truth would surely be.

Dex reached down to touch James' cheek. It was still warm. Life must have ended only moments earlier. Dex choked back a sob, anguish filling his chest as he berated himself for being so slow to come. If he had arrived sooner, surely no longer ago than a quarter hour, he at least could have said good-bye.

"I am so . . . awfully . . . sorry," Dex whispered aloud in the stillness of the musty old shed.

Another tear slipped out of his eye and slid down his cheek.

A matching tear welled bright and wet in the corner of James' right eye.

Dex gasped. Then held a finger gently to the side of James' neck, beneath the jaw shelf where the large artery lay.

He felt the merest hint of movement there, a faint and thready little pulsation of heartbeat on the tip of his finger.

Hope, however, thin, leaped into the back of Dex's throat and a loud, racking sob tore from his mouth.

"Oh, God," Dex blurted. It was not a prayer. Exactly. But it was all he could manage at this moment.

He jumped to his feet and whirled. He needed help. James needed help. And right damned now.

· 13 ·

"You there, boy. No, both of you. Can you help me? I have an injured man back here. He needs a doctor. Is there a doctor here?"

The nearer of the two pimple-faced boys, a youngster with a mottled complexion and soft, doughy build, gave Dex a blank look. The other, shorter and thinner, looked a little more intelligent and was quicker to nod. "We got a doc, mister," that one said.

"I need him. Quickly."

"I dunno that he'd come, mister. He's gen'r'ly busy this time of day, y'know."

"You could help me take my man to the doctor then. Is it far?"

The fat boy shrugged and the lean one hesitated.

"It's worth a dollar to me," Dex said. That seemed to get their attention.

The shorter, dark-haired boy stepped forward with a will once he heard that. "My folks have a hand cart. We could carry him in that."

"Fine. Whatever. Just get it. And quickly. Bring it around behind the deputy's office, in the alley back there. My man is in his shed."

"It's the nigger you mean, mister?" the shorter boy asked. "We heard he was dead."

"He isn't dead, dammit, or he wouldn't need a doctor, would he?"

The fat one shrugged again.

"Go on now. Hurry," Dex prodded.

"I dunno, mister. I think—"

"Listen to me, dammit. I don't care what you think. What I want is for you to get that cart and do what I ask. Quickly."

"You said you'd pay us a dollar?"

"Each. I'll pay you a dollar each. But only if you hurry."

"No matter what?"

"Run, dammit."

The boys turned, finally, and loped out of sight. Dex, too anxious at the moment for anger to take hold, dashed back to James' side to wait for the hand cart and help.

"Is this what you called me out to see? Is this the reason you've made me leave a room full of suffering patients? For a nigger?"

Dex couldn't believe it. Far from expressing concern or beginning the arcane arts of healing, this son of a bitch of a doctor acted . . . indignant. That was the word for it all right. The SOB was offended by the idea of leaving his white patients—a fat old woman and a very pregnant young one—to step outside and see to James.

The doctor was a man of middle years with a bushy mustache and a fine if somewhat aged suit of clothes. His collar was fresh and his tie tidy. Dex's opinion of the man, though, suffered an immediate and downward reconsideration when he saw the contempt with which he looked down his nose at the injured and quite possibly dying James who was bundled awkwardly into a hand cart that was much too small to properly contain him.

"I don't attend to livestock," the doctor announced. "If you want an animal healed . . . not that I see any likelihood of this one surviving, mind you . . . if you want an animal tended, take it to a veterinarian, sir."

"Haven't you heard—"

"Don't wave the law at me, young man. I know what I know, and no law on earth can change the fact that these creatures are not human. They have the physical form of humanity, sir, but lack the spark that is a soul. They are the beasts that lived in the wilderness outside the Garden of Eden, the creatures from whom the children of Adam were required to seek their mates. No damn-yankee lawmaker can alter that truth, sir, so cite me no laws. I'll not stoop to demean my calling by treating such as this."

God, Dex thought. The man was sincere. He really believed . . . wave no laws at him, eh? Dex considered waving something else at the bastard. The muzzle of a gun, say.

Then, bitterly, he realized that would do no good whatsoever. James needed care. Good care. This man might well be capable of giving it, but give it he would not. If under the threat of physical harm he might only see to it that James died instead of tending to James' needs.

Dex swallowed back the rage that threatened to erupt from him. He had no time to give in to useless emotion. Not right now he did not.

"You," Dex said, looking at the thinner of the two boys. "Take him to . . . Jesus, I don't know. Take him to Mr. Barr's house."

Surely Edgar Barr would acquiesce to Dexter's need of a favor. Surely. Please God that he would.

"And tell me where I can find a veterinary surgeon in this town," he added aloud.

"We have no such person here," the doctor advised with a loud sniff and a toss of his impeccably groomed head.

"Then why did you—?"

"Cecil Knott . . . he owns the livery, you may have met him."

Dex nodded.

"He has a way with dumb brutes. Does whatever doctoring is needed on livestock in the vicinity. You might get him to look at the spade. Best do it quickly though. My professional opinion if he was human would be that he won't make it to sundown. But then of course one never knows with the lower orders, does one. They can have amazing vitality, really. Not at all like people in that regard."

Dex wasn't listening to the asshole any longer. He turned and gave the boys orders. "Take him to the Barr residence. There is a carriage shed in the back. Put him in there. Gently, mind. Make a bed of straw for him. One of you . . . you," he pointed to the brighter of the pair, "stay with him and do what you can to make him warm and comfortable. You," he pointed to the other, "go to the door and tell Mrs. Collum what you've done. Tell her Mr. Yancey said to. Can you remember that, boy? My name is Yancey. Tell Mrs. Collum."

"Yessir, I can, 'member."

"Good. Take him now. Quickly. I'll be along in a few minutes with Mr. Knott. Go on now. Go!"

Dex did not bother with any polite good-byes for the doctor. The prick. If he'd spoken at all it only would have been to curse the son of a bitch, and that would have been a waste of time and breath alike.

The boys reluctantly took up the handles of the cart once more—unlike the doctor's, their cooperation was assured. Although they hadn't yet been paid for their services. Dex took off at a run for the livery stable too many blocks away.

• 14 •

"There's not much I can do for him," the livery man said as he knelt beside a comatose James. "Brought some cobweb to stanch wounds with, but all those have clotted over. It was . . . what, yesterday he was beat up?"

"Some time yesterday, yes," Dex said. "I don't know exactly when."

"Doesn't matter," Knott said. "Point is, he made it through the night." The man shook his head. "It's a marvel that he did, and that's for certain sure. I wouldn't of expected him to."

"But he did. Is that a good sign?" Dex asked.

"Could be yes. Could be that it means nothing. He got hit in the head plenty, and I would of thought that would kill him. Since it didn't . . ." Knott shrugged. "Likely he won't die from that. Question now is, what harm was done to his guts. Something gets busted inside a man, it sometimes takes longer for it to kill him." Knott wiped his nose on his shirt sleeve and sniffed. The sniff reminded Dexter of the doctor, damn him anyway, but in Cecil Knott's case it was not a gesture of contempt, simply a matter of having a runny nose.

"I'll tell you what I think," Knott said. "If it was a horse or a goat or something that'd taken a bad fall, say, or got run over by a wagon to get broke up like this, I'd say if it was alive on the third day it'd most likely make it. But before that . . ." He shook his head. "No way to tell. No way to know if he's busted up bad on the inside."

"But you think he has a chance?" Dex persisted.

"A chance, sure. Not much of one maybe, but he has a chance. That's the best I can tell you, mister."

"A chance is all we're asking for right now," Dex said.

The livery man looked up at Dexter and absentmindedly ran the back of his hand under his nose again, then observed, "This boy means more to you than just a servant."

"He's been with me all his life," Dex said, "and all I can remember of mine. We're friends. If you want to make something of that—"

"Not me, mister. It makes no never mind to me. But if I was you, I wouldn't be saying that too often nor too loud around this town."

"I already had that impression."

"Yeah, well, I just thought I'd mention it."

"Thank you."

Knott turned his attention back to James. "Like I already told you, there isn't much I can do for him. He isn't bleeding now. That's the first worry. I'll clean him up a mite and put some balm on the spots where it might do a little good. It's the same ointment I use on the critters that I doctor, but don't think bad about that." He grinned just a little. "This here is also the same stuff I use on my own self."

"All right."

Knott opened the flour sack he'd brought along as his medical kit and pulled out some cotton rags, several different unlabeled jars, a ball of twine and some needles of a size and strength to be used for sewing leather.

"My advice to you, mister," Knott said as he set about the process of cleaning and greasing James' visible wounds, "is to keep him dry and warm. Pile blankets over him. Straw would do if you can't get blankets. Don't worry about waking or feeding him. He needs sleep the most right now. Time to heal and quiet to do it in. Make him comfortable as you can, then sit quiet and wait. If he wakes up hungry, even if it's not for a day or two, that will likely mean he's gonna recover. Not quick though. At the best he won't heal quick. It's gonna take him a long time to come back from a thrashing like this. If he ever does at all."

Dex felt an emptiness in his belly. "You don't think . . . being hit in the head like that, I mean . . . you don't think he could be—"

"Simple?" Again Knott shrugged, his words gruffly matter-of-fact although the hands that were applying a foul-smelling balm to James' wounds were slow and gentle at the task. "I won't make any guesses about that, mister. Could go either way." The man paused in what he was doing and swiveled his head to give Dex a long, slow look before he added, "You want me to make sure he don't wake up? In case you're worried he might be soft in the head now?"

"No!" Dex blurted.

"Good," Knott said. " 'Cause I wouldn't do that sort of thing even if you did want me to. Wouldn't do it to a cow, damn sure wouldn't do it to a human person. Now leave me be while I finish what I'm doing here, will you?"

Dex nodded and forced himself to turn away from his unconscious friend. He still had to pay the boys who'd brought James here, then go offer some explanations and apologies to Mr. Barr.

· 15 ·

Dex woke from a fitful sleep, stretched out on the back seat of the same brougham where a few days earlier—nights, actually—he'd planked that blonde witch Jane whatshername. Something, some unidentified noise, had awakened him and for a brief, hopeful moment he thought it was James who was moving about on his straw pallet nearby.

Instead when he raised up and peered out over the side of the brougham he saw a plump, balding man kneeling beside Dex's still comatose friend.

"Who the hell are you?" Dex demanded as he pulled himself upright and climbed stiff-legged and bleary-eyed down to ground level.

The moment the words left his mouth he regretted the severity of language choice. The man who was beside James had a cherubic look about him. The fellow was round and jolly looking, with a fringe of snowy white hair in a tonsure surrounding his pate and fluffy white Burnside whiskers decorating apple-red cheeks.

He looked, in fact, like a most proper representation of the elf St. Nicholas. Dex guessed he was a priest come to administer last rites or some such as that. "He isn't dead yet," Dex said quickly, before the happy-looking little gent had time to respond to the original, and rude, query.

"So I see." The fat little fellow sighed. He looked, Dex thought, almost . . . disappointed?

"Have you come to pray over him?"

The little man laughed. "Hardly. I was hoping to bury him."

"Hoping?"

"Too strong a term perhaps. I'm sorry about that. Expecting. That is better, isn't it. Expecting to bury him, not hoping."

"You are—?"

"Yonanecker," the jolly elf said with a most charming smile as he rose to his full height—which still put him a good head shorter than Dexter—and extended his hand. "Sam Yonanecker. I'm the undertaker here. Also the barber. And I sell a line of ladies' notions on the side. Catalog items. First class, I must say, and very inexpensive. If you—"

"What are you doing with James there?" Dex demanded.

"That his name? I didn't know. Like I said, I came . . . well . . . expecting to find a client. If you know what I mean."

"We don't need your services," Dex said bluntly.

Yonanecker was unperturbed. "You will," he said cheerfully. "If not mine then the care and attention of someone very much like me. You, your man there, all of us."

Dex shuddered. What Yonanecker said might well be true but, dammit, a man didn't have to *think* about that.

"Will you be burying him here or taking him back home somewhere?" Yonanecker asked.

"I'm not burying him any-damn-place, mister. He isn't dead."

"I didn't mean instantly. If you want him pickled for travel, you see, I shall have to order my supplies. I was thinking I could get a jump on the need if you tell me your requirements in advance. It would make things more, shall we say, *tidy* if I know ahead of time."

"But he isn't dead, dammit." Dex was becoming more than a little exasperated with Yonanecker's happy approach to a most loathsome subject.

"No, I understand that. Just trying to make myself ready to serve your needs, whatever they may be. If you want to know, sir . . . Mr. Yancey isn't it? You may feel better if you become aware that in my youth I sought my fortune in far California. In the gold rush, you see. I found no gold, I confess, but I did find my calling. Apprenticed myself to a man in California named McCarthy. He specialized in providing for the needs of the Celestials who died there. The Chinese, that is to say. For some reason they insisted on being returned to their homeland for burial. Can you imagine that? Fortunately they would pay whatever was asked. It was terribly important to them. McCarthy taught me how to prepare a body to last through months and months of travel at sea. We pickled them. Packed them in hogshead barrels. Started out using grain alcohol, but that isn't nearly so efficacious as you might think. Experience and some barrels broken or leaking enroute taught us that vinegar and certain pickling spices worked ever so much better. And they keep the, um, departed smelling ever so much better when they are, uh, unpacked."

Cherubic. That was the only way to describe Yonanecker's appearance, all right.

Appearances, Dex thought, do truly deceive.

"He isn't dead."

"No, but—"

"I hadn't thought about that, dammit, because he is *not going to die*."

"My dear Mr. Yancey, of course we all die. Someday."

"Not today. All right?"

Yonanecker graced Dexter with another cherubic smile. "Let me know when you do decide. Just in case, that is."

The cheerful little fellow glanced regretfully down at an unconscious James, then went whistling out into the morning light.

Dex took up the cloth and water bottle he'd been using to bathe James' wounds and slightly feverish forehead.

· 16 ·

"Dexter. Come inside now. It won't do you any good to stay out here like this. You'll only make yourself sick too. There is no sense in you suffering along with him."

Dex looked up at the man who was his host. Dex's eyes burned and his neck itched furiously from the beard stubble that continued to accumulate there. He had been out here in the shed beside James for . . . what now? Two nights and two days. Something like that. He was a trifle hazy on the exact amount of time. Not that it mattered. He shook his head.

"You have to eat, Dexter. Come inside."

"No, Mr. Barr. I . . . he might need me. He might wake up. When he does, sir, I want to be here."

"He won't know if you are here or not, Dexter."

"But I know, Mr. Barr. And there's something else that I know, too. If it was the other way around, if it was me lying there all beat and hurting and near to death . . . if it was me down there on that pallet, James would be right here at my side."

Barr gave Dex a pitying look. Then he said, "I will have Mrs. Collum fetch out something hot." He wrinkled his nose and added, "And a wash basin would be in order too, I think."

"Sorry, sir."

"No no, son, you . . . do whatever it is you feel you need to do. You are welcome to the use of whatever I have for as long as you need it. I hope you know that."

"Yes sir, and I thank you deeply, sir."

"Yes, well, we will talk again later." The old man smiled. "After you've had time to bathe perhaps."

And at that the gentleman was being polite. He was not the only one capable of distinguishing scents, and Dex by now was a good day and a half past being fully ripe.

Dex thanked Mrs. Collum for the tray. Without getting too close to her. Offending her would be bad enough. At this point he was fearful that his odor might knock her down, and what would he do if he found himself with two patients in the carriage shed needing tending.

An exaggeration perhaps, but . . . ah! His thoughts were diverted and swept completely away by a positively heavenly aroma when he lifted the tea towel Mrs. Collum had laid over the tray.

The meal was hardly Spartan. She'd delivered it and made a swift escape back into the house but surely there was nothing missing that he might have wanted in addition to all this.

She'd prepared a small carafe of steaming hot coffee already laced with thick cream. There was a marvelously aromatic soup with flecks of chive and tiny dumplings bobbing in a clear broth. Grits. A beef and potato hash minced extra fine. Home canned peaches preserved with cinnamon and clove. Biscuits. Thick sausage gravy.

His mouth watered furiously as one smell after another came to him off the heavy tray.

It occurred to him that everything she'd prepared here was soft and easily chewed. Perhaps she thought he was the one who'd been battered. Mmm, no. She knew better. Even so she'd made up a tray suitable for an invalid, quite probably without consciously thinking about it.

No matter. Dex set the tray on the floor of the brougham that was his bed, parlor and now dining area, then perched on the running board while he sorted out the napkins and silverware provided.

He was looking forward to this. Hadn't realized just how ravenous he'd become during his vigil.

He picked up a spoon and dipped it into the soup.

Then whirled, all thought of food forgotten, as behind him he heard a low, plaintive groan from the pallet where James lay.

James's hand twitched. His right knee lifted and his head rolled fitfully to the left, then right and back again.

Those were the first signs of life he'd shown since Dex found him virtually discarded in that shed behind the deputy's office.

He was alive, by God. He was alive!

· 17 ·

"Can you hear me? You had me worried, you son of a bitch. Damn you. If you can hear me, wiggle your ears."

Dex wasn't sure but he thought, would almost have sworn, that the corner of James' mouth twitched. It wasn't much, but Dex took it as a grin and his spirits soared.

The livery man—just wait until he told James that he'd been tended to by a vet, and an unschooled one at that—had said if he was still alive on the third day there was a good chance he would recover. Well this was the third morning, by damn, and James was still here.

Dex got water and a rag and very carefully and gently bathed James's face and eyes and mouth in an effort to wipe away some of the pus that had accumulated. Most of the dried blood was gone, taken care of by several days of repeated washing, but the pus formed anew in the swollen mess that had been made of James' eyes and mouth. Lord only knew what they'd used to beat his face like that. Dex felt fairly sure James' teeth were loose and he might yet lose some, but for the time being they were still in place. He supposed that could be taken as a victory. Sort of.

"You were ugly enough to start with," Dex chattered aimlessly as he continued to bathe James' more obvious wounds.

"This isn't gonna make you any better looking."

James' lips moved just a little. Dex leaned close but could not make out whatever it was his friend was trying to whisper.

Not that it mattered. Not a lick, by damn.

James was alive. He was aware. He could hear and he could respond.

That was what counted.

There would be time enough later on for James to tell Dex whatever it was he wanted to say.

God, Dex would listen by the hour if it would make James feel any better.

He'd still tease and belittle him, of course. But hell, James would think there was something wrong if he didn't.

The good news was that James would live. The rest of it was mere detail, and they would think about that some other time.

· 18 ·

"Wiggle my ears." The whisper was faint and slow but the words were clearly discernible. "You son of a bitch."

Dex grinned and spooned another few drops of the aromatic broth into James' mouth. "I kinda thought that would get you."

James' lips moved. Again he was trying to smile.

There had been a time when they'd been boys . . . they were eight, nine years old perhaps . . . when Dex had discovered he could wiggle his ears. And James found that he could not.

James had spent hours back then concentrating. Moving his jaw this way and that. Frowning. Scowling. Contorting his face, even his entire upper body in every direction and in every way he could imagine.

None of it ever caused his ears to wiggle.

His eyebrows practically danced. His mouth formed itself into shapes God never intended. But his ears? Nothing.

And Dex would infuriate him anew upon each and every failure by laughing happily and oh so easily wiggling his own ears in full view of a humiliated James.

James never *had* learned to wiggle them actually. Although he had learned not to try. At least when Dexter might catch him in the attempt.

"Son of a bitch," James whispered again now. The words were sweet to hear, Dex concluded.

"Hush your talking, black boy, and take some more of this here soup. I swear, boy, you mo' trouble than you wu'th." Dex smiled and wielded the spoon with tender care.

James' expression, what little there was of it beneath the swelling and the abrasions, changed and he shook his head very slightly to reject Dex's latest attempt at feeding him. "Dex."

"I'm here, James. What is it?"

"I . . . I'm sorry. God knows I'm sorry."

"You didn't do anything wrong and you don't have to apologize for anything. Now be quiet and take some more of this broth, will you? You need to get some food in you if you're gonna heal."

"No, I . . . our money. I should have . . . I don't know. I should have protected it better. I'm sorry, Dex, I swear I am."

Dex carefully emptied a spoonful of broth into James' mouth, then tugged at the waistband of his friend's trousers, lifting the cloth away from James' body a few inches. There was nothing inside James' britches there but dark flesh.

"I'll be damned," he said.

"You didn't know?"

Dex shrugged, then realized James couldn't see that gesture since his eyes were still swollen closed. "Never gave it any thought, actually. I was afraid . . . I hate to say this, but the truth is I was scared you were gonna up and die on me." He lightened up on the tone of voice and said, "That wouldn't have been so bad except I'm the one who would have to go back to Louisiana and tell your mama. And she'd be right pissed off if I went and let somebody kill her only child."

"But our money, Dexter. I let them take all our money."

"Don't worry about it. We'll think of something." Dex fed his friend another tiny swallow of broth, picking carefully through the bowl so as to spoon up nothing except the clear liquid. The little dumplings and bit of floating things looked soft but he did not want to take any chances on what James could or, much worse, could not handle just yet. James seemed still pretty shaky on the subject of accepting nourishment.

"If nothing else," Dex said lightly, "we'll find the gents that did this to you and ask for our money back. You, uh, don't happen to remember who they were, do you?"

James tried to shake his head but only winced and gasped in pain from the effort.

"It's all right," Dex said quickly. "You don't have to think about it."

"Hell, white boy, I been thinking about almost nothing else ever since I woke up."

"And they were—?"

"There was five of them. I can tell you that much."

"Would you recognize them if you saw them again?"

"Dexter, I never saw them the first time."

"But you just said—"

"They were wearing masks. Hoods, you might say. Decorated masks. Green cloth with crazy shapes sewn on to make crazy faces on the masks. Red, black, yellow, darker green. I saw the masks. I got no idea who was wearing them."

"Would you recognize the masks if you saw them again?"

"Damn right I would. I'd recognize every one of those offay cocksuckers if ever I saw them again." James' voice was stronger now as anger fueled and intensified his words.

"Then we'll just have to think of some way we can get you a second chance to meet the hooded gentlemen, won't we?"

"That'd be fine, Dexter, but don't expect me to stand still for them a second time."

"Won't either one of us be standing idle if there's a second time, James. I promise you that."

"Dexter."

"Yes, James?"

"Shut up, will you? I'm kinda tired out. Think I'm gonna take me a little nap now if you'll be quiet an' leave me be."

The whispered words were barely past James' lips before his breathing steadied and slowed, and a faint, rasping snore began to drone through the carriage house.

◆ 19 ◆

Dex withdrew behind the brougham. He did not expect James to awaken soon but certainly did not want to risk the slightest chance that James might see what he was doing there lest it create guilt to add to James' other problems— and there investigated the rather meager contents of his own pockets.

Sixty-two dollars. He'd already paid the hotel bill, but he still owed Cecil Knott for boarding the horses. And they still had to have something to live on.

Sixty two dollars would be enough to keep them in food for a fairly considerable period. Or so Dex supposed. He sighed. Money worries really were not something he'd ever had to cope with. He'd been raised a Southern gentleman, son of a slaveholder, scion of a plantation family.

All of that had come crashing down. And only now was he beginning to realize just how far down, just how thorough the change had been.

Even when circumstance, fraternal jealousies, and certain events that might be misunderstood before a court of law forced him to leave his home forever behind him he hadn't thought things would come to . . . this.

Sixty-two dollars. And no prospects of gaining more.

Dex grunted. Poverty was not something he'd particularly aspired to. It was not a state he would welcome now.

Fortunately, it was not something he had to concern himself with at this exact moment.

Good-hearted Mr. Barr would not think of asking a guest for payment, nor would the old gentleman be capable of turning a Yancey away from his home.

That was one good thing. Dex could be assured of an extended and quite genuine welcome with his father's old school chum.

As for the future . . . Dex had no idea what the lower classes did when it came to providing themselves with the necessities of life. Like women. And brandy. And women.

How could a poor man even be expected to clothe himself properly? Dex shuddered. He had a shirt that was beginning to fray at the cuff. He'd intended to have a replacement tailored when they got to Austin. But what did a decent shirt cost nowadays? He had no idea because never in his life had he been required to buy one. There had always been someone on the plantation—slave or employee, the distinction hardly mattered as to the skills available—ready to make one up whenever he wished.

The same would apply when it came to trousers and smallclothes. Those that he had were in good repair, of course. But what would he do when eventually they had to be replaced?

He would have to turn to strangers, of course. And he would have to pay for the services.

What about shaving? A shave was not particularly expensive. But it had to be done every day or nearly so. As simple a thing as shaving meant a constant requirement for cash.

He supposed he could buy a razor and learn to shave himself. But . . . dammit . . . the truth was that he did not *want* to shave himself.

For that matter—in fact, very much the moreso once he thought about it—Dexter Lee Yancey did not *want* to scramble for a livelihood.

He, and James too, would have to find some acceptable means of providing for themselves.

In the past there had been gambling profits to count on. But that was when they'd had a deceptively fast racing mule to count on.

Dex would have been happy enough to make a living with the pasteboards as a fair number of disinherited sons seemed to do. But the simple truth was that while he enjoyed card games well enough, he was not especially good at playing them. Gaming was an amusement for him. It was most assuredly not a potential source of reliable income.

He could fence quite well and shoot with great accuracy if not speed. But he rather doubted he could find much potential in those gentlemanly attributes.

He quite enjoyed the pleasures and the company of the ladies, including—or even especially—so-called ladies of the night. He just plain liked them. But he had no illusions that a career as a pimp or whoremaster would satisfy him. Dex's father would turn over in his grave at that prospect, and his brother Lewis who'd wrested control of Blackgum Bend plantation would likely die of apoplexy induced by social mortification if ever he heard about anything like that.

Dex smiled just a little. If the thought really would kill Lewis . . . But no, probably it would not. Drat the luck.

The truth was that Dex had no clue which way to turn from this point. Until now pretty much the whole of his life had been a lark even if a sometimes knobby one.

Good Lord! Surely he wasn't going to have to actually grow up.

He made a sour face and put his concerns for the future aside to be picked at later.

Right now the thing before him was to see to James' recovery.

And to the little matter of retribution for the infliction of those injuries.

Dexter might not know much about the various means by which a man could make his livelihood, but he knew quite a lot about vengeance.

Someone else, or more precisely at least five someones here in Wharburton, Texas, would receive instruction in Dex's views on that subject.

· 20 ·

Dex did not feel comfortable with the idea of leaving James alone during the next several days. Not until most of the swelling had gone down around his eyes and he could see again.

It wasn't so much that James needed constant attention for his healing. Far from it. The best healing agent was and probably always would be simple sleep, Dex figured.

But he was worried about what might happen if James were left unguarded.

It seemed entirely possible that if someone was serious enough about trying to kill him in the first place they might very well come back with the idea of doing a better job of mayhem once they learned that their intended victim was still living. Which they most assuredly must know by now. After all, Sam Yonanecker had already given up his prospects of employment for the burying, at least for the moment. Yonanecker was a frequent visitor to Edgar Barr's carriage house for the first few days, only to ultimately concede defeat. With a fatalistic shrug and a small smile he acknowledged that James very likely would live after all. At least he was gracious enough to omit the "better luck next time" that Dex fully expected to hear from the man.

In any event, Yonanecker's disappointment was certain to be public knowledge. And therefore so was James' survival.

Dex did not want to risk allowing the sons of bitches who'd done this to come back and improve on their previous sloppy performance, so until James' eyes were open and he could at least see to defend himself—albeit from flat on his back—Dex remained virtually at his side except for an occasional foray inside Barr's house for food and a trip to the outhouse now and then.

With the benefit of broth, cornmeal mush, and mashed potatoes heavily laced with rich gravy, though, James was making fair progress at recovery.

When Dex thought that progress had come sufficiently far, he dragged James into a corner of the carriage house and propped him up so he could easily see if anyone opened the door and tried to come inside.

"You've probably already thought about this," Dex admitted, "but this is my fault a lot more'n it's yours."

"How do you figure that, white boy?" James still looked like hell. And would have looked even worse if his dark skin coloring didn't minimize the extent of the awful bruising.

"We talked weeks ago about the fact that you oughta have a gun handy. It's my fault that I didn't buy you one right off. If you'd been carrying a gun that day—"

"Then they probably would've shot me instead of just beating the hell out of me. Have you thought about that?"

"No, I—"

"Stop looking for ways to make yourself out to be guilty of something here. It wasn't your fault," James said. "For that matter, dammit, it wasn't mine either. It just happened, that's all. As for the gun, well, the fact of the matter is that I didn't have one. Neither one of us will ever know for sure if things would have gone differently if I'd had a pistol in my pocket."

"From now on you will," Dex told him. He took out his own small but finely crafted .32 rimfire revolvers and laid both of them onto James' lap. "These aren't powerful, but they're accurate." He smiled. "Of course you aren't as good a shot as me, but—"

"I'll notch your ears for you slick as grease on ice and you know it," James returned.

"That'll be the day." The truth was that James was an excellent shot with rifle or revolver either one, very nearly as accomplished as Dexter himself with gun or sword. But then they'd been practicing with and cheerfully competing against each other their whole lives long, so it should have come as no surprise for anyone to discover this if they ever gave it thought.

"You shouldn't give me both your pistols, Dex. What are you gonna carry?"

"I've been thinking about that. It won't matter so much if folks discover I'm armed. It's apt to stir some resentments if they see a black man wearing guns, so you can take both of these. They hide easy under a coat or in a pocket, and they're fine guns. As for me, I'm going to get something with some more oomph to it. A .45 maybe."

James managed a smile. "There goes the cut of your coat, you know, unless you have new clothes tailored."

Dex did not mention the state of their finances. But there was no way they could afford a new suit of clothes for him. He either had to learn to live with an ill-fitting coat—and what a dim and dreary prospect that would be—or carry his weapons in the open. No contest there, of course.

"Do you need anything?" he asked. "I'm going to go downtown and buy myself some replacements for those."

"I'll be all right." James lightly touched the checkered walnut grips of the little .32s as if to reassure Dex—or himself—and nodded.

"How about some codeine or laudanum or such?"

"Don't bother. The pain isn't half what it was to start with."

Dex nodded. "I won't be long."

James's lips parted in a grin that was made more than a little lopsided by the swelling there. "I expect I'll be here when you get back."

Dex grunted and strode away from the makeshift hospital that Mr. Barr's carriage house had become.

• 21 •

Apparently the town of Wharburton thought of itself as being less violent than it really was. At any rate it did not support a gunsmith shop. It took Dex several inquiries before he was directed to a store that advertised hardware and farm implements and which also proved to offer a limited selection of firearms for sale, most of them shotguns.

"Sure, I have some pistols," the proprietor responded to Dexter's request. "In fact, if you can get along with cap and ball, I can make you a real good price." The man sighed. "Brand new ones, mister, still in the factory grease."

"Progress catch you unaware?" Dex asked.

"You could sure say that. Everybody wanted the Colt Army model revolving pistol. Damn factory couldn't keep up with demand hardly, and I couldn't get any. So I made a deal with an outfit over in N'Orleans that tooled up during the war an' then couldn't sell all their guns because the damn Yankees captured the city. Still had crates of them, and they made me what I thought was a bargain. How the hell was I to know that Colt would be coming out with a cartridge model?" He shook his head sadly.

Dex thought of several ways the man might have become suspicious about that. Reading, for instance. But he did not think it prudent to mention that aloud. "I'll be wanting the cartridge model myself, thank you."

"All right. I got 'em, mister. Twenty two dollars apiece. How many do you want?"

Dex whistled. That seemed awfully steep. When he said so the hardware man only shrugged. "That's the factory recommended price, mister. You want me to show you the catalog they send out for us dealers?"

"No, thanks. I believe you. I was just . . . that seems an awful lot. Especially since I was wanting two pistols."

"You figure to kill a lot of folks, do you?" the storekeeper said with a little laugh.

Dex laughed too. It seemed more sensible than giving a truthful answer to what was obviously a humorous rhetorical question.

But the truth, of course, was: Yes, he did indeed intend to kill or maim a fair number of local citizens, thank you.

Instead he only chuckled and said, "I travel a lot, you see, and a man never knows what he'll run into on the road."

"That's true enough. But the price is still twenty-two dollars each."

"I can't spend that much," Dex admitted, that comment being all too truthful.

"You too proud to carry a gun that's been used? Or anyways carried by somebody else?"

"No, sir. Not if they work."

"Tell you what then. Last summer there was a fellow came in and made me a swap. He wanted some of the Colt Peacemaker model, just like 'most everybody does. Had a pair of Webleys to give in trade."

"I never heard of such a gun," Dex said honestly.

"English made, they are. Built strong and they shoot just fine . . . I know for I carried them down along the riverbank and fired off a few shots out of each before I'd make the trade . . . but they aren't pretty guns like the Colt is. They look kinda blocky and rough. But they aren't crude. Just . . . different looking." He hesitated for a moment, then added,

"The man I got them from said that damn Yankee general, you know the one, that Custer that got himself and a helluva lot of bluebelly soldiers chopped up by the Indians a few years ago, this fella said that Custer himself favored the Webley. Said that's what he was carrying when he made his famous Last Stand." The fellow laughed. "Not that I'd call that much of an endorsement, but if you admired the man—"

Dex made a face. "Can't say as I can work up much in the way of admiration for a Yankee, but I suppose that one did know more than a little about guns. I expect I'd take a look at these Webleys you've got."

"One more thing I got to tell you. You can't buy ammunition for them just every place like you can for the Colt. These English guns have a big enough bore. They're .455. Almost the same as the Colt but not an exact fit."

"You have ammunition to go with them?"

"I do. Came to me in the same trade. Got the two guns, holsters to carry them, and three boxes of cartridges less what I shot out there by the river that time."

"All right, mister. Let me see them, then if I think they'll do we can find out if we can come to terms for them."

"Friend, I can damn near guarantee you that we'll make a deal for they're doing me no good at all laying in a box back there. In fact, I'd throw in an entire crate of those Confederate cap and ball pistols if you talk real fast."

Dex laughed. "Just the Webleys, I think."

• 22 •

The fact that James was capable now of fending for himself a bit gave Dex a sense of freedom that was positively exhilarating after the days of enforced idleness. After he showed off his new revolvers and fed James his supper, Dex walked through the garden to the Barr house to partake of the quite remarkable if all too often taken-for-granted pleasures of a tub bath and a sit-down meal complete with wine, fine china, and a brandy in Mr. Barr's study afterward.

"You've been remarkably faithful to your manservant, Dexter. I admire that. Your father would be proud of you," the old gentleman offered along with a good quality but somewhat overly dry cigar.

"If I remember correctly, sir, you yourself have strong convictions when it comes to taking care of one's people. I remember Papa talking about you after the war. He'd had a letter from you, I believe, and he was saying how he wished he could keep on all our Blackgum Bend folk the way you were doing here at Windthistle. He couldn't, though. He kept those he could and pensioned off the old darkies, but there were some that he just couldn't afford to employ. It . . . everything changed after the war, of course. But I know that was one of the changes that hurt Papa. He hated having to tell his people they would have to leave. Did you continue to employ yours for all these years, Mr. Barr?"

The old man looked away, and Dex thought but was not certain that his expression had turned sad, perhaps with memories of a better past.

"I'm sorry, sir. It was not my intend to intrude. If I've been rude, sir, please accept my apology."

Barr looked at him again. "No apology is necessary, Dexter. I just wish . . ." He sighed. "I tried to continue. Lord knows that I did. But last year I had to let them go. All of them."

"All, sir? But what about—?"

"Windthistle is barren, Dexter. The fields are fallow and the shanties falling to ruin. Those that remain. I suppose many have been dismantled by now for building materials or for firewood."

No wonder he'd looked sad, Dex thought. Fallow! Dex would scarcely be capable of imagining such a thing at Blackgum Bend. He did not want to see such a thing, not even in his own mind's eye.

"To tell you the truth, son, I haven't had the heart to drive out there these past few months. I haven't seen it since last spring, and God willing I'll never have to look at those useless fields again. If there is one thing I can be grateful for it is having moved to town during my wife's final years. She wanted to be close to friends and the doctor, you see, else we probably would have stayed in the big house at Windthistle and I would long ago have completed the task you interrupted a few days ago."

"Is that why . . . that is . . ." Dex felt his cheeks begin to burn. He'd blurted the question without thinking, and as soon as the words left his tongue he knew how awful they sounded.

And of course the ruin of all he'd worked to build throughout his entire life was what prompted Mr. Barr to attempt suicide. Men killed themselves every day for reasons far less genuine than that one.

"Yes," Barr answered with calm simplicity.

"Is there anything I can do, sir?"

"Nothing, Dexter. I am afraid there is nothing anyone can do." The elderly gentleman gave Dex a wan smile. "It is kind of you to offer."

"Yes, sir. I, uh, I think I should be getting back now to check on my man."

"Of course." Barr stood, smiled, extended his hand to Dexter. "Thank you for the pleasure of your company this evening, Dexter. I hope now that your manservant can be left to himself you will make it your practice to take your meals with me. And Mrs. Collum is making up your bed. She will show you to your room when you return."

"You are very kind, sir."

Barr waved the thanks away. "Your father never failed me in all the years of our friendship, Dexter. I will do no less for his son than he would have done for mine had I been so blessed."

"Yes, sir. Thank you, sir." When he left, Dex was not entirely sure if he were making an exit . . . or an escape.

But the prospect of a soft bed with clean linen and room to stretch his legs was plenty enticing. He would sit up with James a while longer this evening, but he would definitely come back to the house when he was ready to retire for the night.

· 23 ·

God but Dex did love light, baking powder biscuits, especially when they were swimming in a good and greasy milk and sausage gravy. Mrs. Collum made biscuits so light they likely would have floated off the plate if it hadn't been for the weight of the gravy. He belched, pondered, decided he could hold just one more, and reached for it.

"May I be honest with you, Mr. Barr?" he asked when the last drop and morsel were finally disposed of and Mrs. Collum was busy clearing the soiled plates away.

"I hope you always shall be, Dexter."

"I suspect it will come as no surprise to you, sir, if I tell you that I intend to have satisfaction from the men who nearly killed my man James."

"Of course I can understand your intentions, Dexter. Any gentleman would be inclined to take the incident as an assault upon himself. But I hope you'll not put yourself in harm's way for the sake of a servant."

"I appreciate your advice, sir, but it is more than that." It wasn't, actually, but Dex had no intention of elaborating about the friendship between himself and a black man. "Apart from the beating, the scoundrels robbed me. Not my man. Me." Dex explained about their theory that no one would be apt to suspect James of carrying a large sum of money.

"I appreciate the idea behind your decision, Dexter, but I must say that you've given some brigand the pleasure of an unexpectedly good haul."

"So I have," Dex admitted.

"You do know that you are unlikely to recover any of the money even if you learn who battered your man."

"Yes, sir, but there are many more kinds of recompense than money. And most of them, I should say, are more important than mere lucre."

"Quite right," Barr agreed.

"I've been able to speak with my man, however, and he never saw the faces of his attackers. He wouldn't be able to identify them. But I was hoping, since you know the local climate, sir, I was hoping you might give me some idea of how to approach this matter. You see, while James did not see their faces, the five who attacked him were all wearing hoods. Distinctive hoods at that. He is certain he would be able to recognize those."

Mr. Barr went suddenly pale and for a moment Dex thought he was having palpitations or some sort of seizure.

"Sir?" Dex leaped from his chair and raced around the table to crouch by the old man's side. "Sir? Are you all right, sir?" Dex reached for a glass of water, dipped one corner of a napkin into it, and bathed Barr's face. After a few moments the color began to return to Barr's complexion and his breathing seemed easier again.

"I am . . . thank you, Dexter. I'm fine now. Really."

"Yes, sir." Dex was not so sure about that, but he dropped the damp napkin onto the table and returned to his own seat. Mr. Barr nodded, took in a deep breath, and gulped down some of the now cooling coffee left from their breakfast.

"I am sorry if I worried you, son. It is just . . . do you remember what we were speaking of last night?"

"About Windthistle? Yes, of course I do, sir."

"It was . . . the same group of men who beat your man are the ones responsible for the failure of Windthistle. Your mention of them . . . I'm afraid it startled me, Dexter. They are . . . evil. That is the only way to describe them. Evil. And no one knows who they really are. They've ruined me. Driven all my people away. Many others too, of course. They've nearly ruined every planter along this stretch of the Trinity River. They are Satan's spawn, Dexter, and my advice to you, young man, is for you to take your man and leave Wharburton the very first moment that he is able to travel. But please, Dexter. Please do not even consider opposing them. They would murder you without compunction. They don't confine their terror to the niggers, you see. No one can prove it . . . no one wants to prove it, such is the power of their sway here . . . but those people have murdered more than one white man in this county already. I'd not like to see Charles Yancey's son become their next victim."

"You say you don't know who they are, sir?"

"No. They are secretive. They shy away from sunlight and honesty the very same way bats and vampires are said to do and for the same reasons, I suppose. They'd not be able to withstand the scrutiny of honest men. But that is beside the point, Dexter. I want you to leave here just as quickly as you are able."

"Sir."

"Yes?"

"Your advice is well intentioned. I know that. But will you tell me what you can of these men?"

"All I know of them, Dexter, is the name they collectively call themselves. They are the Knights of the Ku Klux Klan, Dexter, and they are as evil as their Satanic master. I know . . ." He shook his head. "I can't tell you more than that, son. I am not honestly certain that I would tell you even if I knew more."

The Klan? Dex was as badly jolted by that accusation as old Mr. Barr seemed to be.

But for a very different reason.

He knew well the Knights of the Klan, and a finer group of men he'd never met.

And now . . . here . . . this was not right. This was not at all as it should have been.

"If you will excuse me, sir? I need to see to James."

"Of course."

Dex pushed back from the table and turned toward the dining room door.

"Dexter."

"Yes, sir?"

"Remember what I told you. Leave Wharburton the very moment you are able. Will you do that for me? Please?"

Dex left the old man without making any promises. Not because he was unwilling but because he was unable.

He *would* have satisfaction. And God willing he would defend the integrity and the honor of the Knights as well.

• 24 •

"Damn but you offay white boys are lazy," James observed late that afternoon. "I mean, I got me a reason to be lounging about in broad daylight. I'm hard at work a'healing from what all's been done to me. But you? You don't have such an excuse, and you've done no more work than I have to-day."

"Just what sort of work would you expect me to do?" Dex asked without bothering to open his eyes. There was a shaft of slanting afternoon sunlight all too close to his face, and he had his hat propped over his nose in order to block out the annoyance. The inside of his hat smelled musty but not to the point of being rancid. Quite.

"Hell, I don't know. You could chop some cotton. Heft a bale. Haul a barge. Anything to make money. You got to support me, you know. It's your obligation. What us darkies call noblesse oblige."

"That's what you call it, is it?"

"Where I come from it is, yeah."

"It occurs to me that you put on airs from time to time, boy. Gonna have to show you the whip now and then. Keep you in line."

James laughed. "That will be the day. On my worst day I could whup your lily-white ass, and you know it."

"Care to try it now?" Dex offered.

"I would but I'm trying to catch up on my sleep."

"Seriously, James, how are you doing?"

"Better. No, I mean it. There's less pain in my belly, and I can move my legs a little now without it hurting so bad. I had no idea how often a man uses the muscles down around his stomach. Just trying to sit up or lift your foot off the blanket means you have to use those, and to tell you the truth they were hurting like hell. I think one of them must have kicked me in the belly. It's a lot better now, particularly my gut. Mind you, I wouldn't want to be walking around without help yet. But I think this evening I'll be able to make it to the backhouse if I can lean on you."

"That will be a relief. It isn't seemly for a gentleman of my breeding to be hauling a slop bucket for the likes of you."

"Wouldn't hardly be seemly for me to be leaning all over you neither, but I sure as hell hope that won't stop you from letting me go take a shit in a decent sitting position for a change. Jeez but I hate that thunder mug."

"We'll wait until after dark. I don't think Mr. Barr and Mrs. Collum would be surprised if they did see, but we don't want to risk making ourselves unwelcome just in case."

"You got any ideas about how we're going to get some money in our pockets again?" James asked.

Dex chuckled and, pushing the hat onto his head, sat upright. "You accuse me of lazing about this afternoon, but in fact I do have a few ideas that I've come up with today."

"Anything I can help with?"

"No. This isn't the sort of thing that a black man can accomplish other than to make things worse. All you have to do is lay back and get the rest of your healing done."

"Thank God," James said with great sincerity. "This time I'm happy to turn everything over to you entire."

· 25 ·

"Mr. Barr. May I disturb you for a moment, sir?"

The old gentleman nodded and beckoned Dexter into his study. He was seated in his favorite chair with a cup of coffee steaming at his side and a book open in his lap. "It's always a pleasure to see you, my boy."

"Thank you, sir." Dex dropped into the chair close to Mr. Barr's and waved away an offer of coffee or of something stronger. "I'm fine, sir, thank you. What I would like, if you don't mind, is to ask a few questions."

"Of course."

"It occurred to me, sir, that yesterday you mentioned something about those hooded men, the Klansmen that is, ruining you and other planters along the Trinity."

"That's correct, Dexter, although I am sorry to say it. I am ruined and unfortunately I am not the only one."

"If you don't mind me asking, sir, how is it that this has happened. That is . . . how have they gone about it?"

Mr. Barr sighed. "I gather that it is an unintended consequence of their evil, Dexter, but not their principal desire. These men, Klansmen you call them, hate the Negroes. They also seem to hate Jews, Mexicans, Gypsies, any and everyone who is not demonstrably white and Christian."

Dex fidgeted a little in his chair but kept his mouth shut. This was Mr. Barr's account to tell, and Dex did not want to intrude upon the telling of it. Even if he found it difficult to agree with what the old man was saying.

"Perhaps two years ago the Klan became a powerful force in Wharburton. It was not unknown before that time, but in the past it was far from being the menace that it has since become."

Dex nodded and remained silent.

"Then . . . as I said, it would have been about two years gone . . . then the hooded men became very vigorous and violent in the pursuit of their hatred and evil. Night riding became common. Crosses were burned, and that quickly progressed to whippings, beatings, even to hangings.

"Negroes from one end of the county to the other were issued warnings. They were told to leave or to suffer the consequences of refusal. At first there was fear, but very few left. A few families . . . those who had children to fret about and were the most vulnerable . . . a few left at once." Mr. Barr took a swallow of his coffee, frowned and went to the sideboard to get a decanter of brandy that he used to fortify the coffee. Apparently he was finding his tale a difficult one to relate.

"The ones who packed up and ran were the smart ones," he said when he went on again. "After the warnings the violence increased. Men were strung up by their wrists and lashed with whips. Women, even little girls, were stripped naked and raped while their husbands and sons and brothers were required to watch. Then the men and boys were beaten, too.

"Any who tried to defend themselves were hanged. Or worse. I know of one man who was hanged by his thumbs and then whipped quite literally to death. I am told he was cut up as if with knives."

Mr. Barr shook his head sadly. "It is evil, Dexter. Pure evil what these men do. And of course the result was obvious. The people were told to leave. Those who remained alive, left.

"Most of the hired hands on the plantations were niggers, of course. Within six months of the start of it all, they were gone.

"Then the night riders began visiting the Mexicans who lived and worked here. The warnings were repeated. I doubt you could find a single Mexican living in this entire county today.

"We had a Jew who lived in town. A good man, kind and thoughtful and decent. They warned him to leave or see his daughter raped in front of him. He spoke with me before he left. He offered me his property for a pittance. I wished . . . by that time I was in deep financial straits myself. My hands were all gone and my crops rotting with no one to pick them. I hadn't money to give him. He found no one who would buy. The decent folks either had no money, as I did, or they were fearful that the Klansmen wanted Aaron's property for themselves. Eventually he simply drove away. He abandoned everything he'd worked his whole life to build. He was a good man. The community will suffer from his loss. But what choice did he have? He, the Mexicans, the niggers . . . the Klan drove them all away, drove many of us into poverty when they did so.

"Surely they understand this, Dexter. Surely they are aware of the damage they cause. Why do they continue their evil? Will they keep on until they completely destroy this community and themselves along with it?"

Dex had no answers to give.

But at least now he knew a little more about the men who came so very near to killing James.

"I think, sir, if you don't mind, I would like to join you in a brandy," Dex said.

Mr. Barr looked grateful for the change of subject. He nodded and let Dex pour for both of them.

♦ 26 ♦

"I thought you were gonna be out laying waste to Klansmen left and right this afternoon," James said when Dex returned to the carriage house. His voice was thin and reedy. But it was a sight better than it had been. Dex thought that an encouraging sign.

"I was. Sort of," Dex told him.

"Don't try to bullshit me, white boy. I may be banged up but it wasn't my brain they beat on. From this corner I can see out that door over there, and I can hear just as good as ever. You've been in Mr. Barr's house." He lifted his chin a fraction of an inch and rather loudly sniffed. "I'd say you been over there drinking."

"You're guessing. You couldn't possibly smell my breath from that far away."

James grinned, confirming Dex's statement but pleased with himself about the accuracy of his guesswork.

"I been learning things."

"Interesting?" James asked.

"Not so much interesting as useful. Maybe."

"Can I ask what you have in mind?"

Dex shrugged. "I'd tell you if I knew, James. Fact is, I'm not for sure myself where I'm going with this. But . . . there's

a lot that I'm hearing from Mr. Barr that doesn't sound right
to me."

"About those men in the hoods?"

"About them, I suppose. About the Klan mostly," Dex
said.

"How so?"

Again Dexter had no good answer to give. He thought
about it for a moment, then shook his head. "It's a gut feeling," he finally answered. "There's something here . . . I
can't quite decide what . . . that doesn't seem right to me. Of
course this is Texas. What I know about comes from back
home in Louisiana and along the Mississippi. Could be that
things are different here."

James snorted. "I can damn well tell you that things are
different here. Back home I wasn't thought of as anything
more than a dumb-ass field nigger, but at least there wasn't
anybody beating up on me for it. As long as I used a little
common sense I could walk around and not have to worry
who was standing in the shadows behind me."

"From now on, James, don't take any shit off anybody.
Not white, black, brown, or green. Somebody comes at you
again, pull those pistols and let fly."

"And get my neck stretched from a tall oak tree," James
said.

"The second part of my advice to you, my friend, is to
run like hell just as quick as the shooting stops."

James grinned again. "Now you're starting to make
sense." He cocked his head and peered up at Dex who was
fidgeting with his clothes, feeling to make sure the bow of
his tie was straight and the strings of equal length. "You
going somewhere again so soon?" he asked.

"Uh huh," Dex told him. "Think I'm gonna go out and
get drunk tonight."

"Yeah, that's always a good thing for a man when he's
broke and not sure what else to do."

"My philosophy exactly," Dex said cheerfully. "Don't wait
up for me, hear?" He settled his hat at a jaunty angle and

patted his waist to make sure the stout Webley revolvers were in place, one in plain sight to the left of his belt buckle where it could be reached with either hand and the other tucked less conspicuously into the hollow of his back.

"Let me know it's you when you come staggering home," James suggested, "so I won't make a mistake and shoot your nuts off."

"I'll try to remember that," Dex said. "Is there anything you need?"

"Yeah. About five hundred miles between me and this town."

"We'll work on that. But not right now." Dex winked at his friend and ambled out into the waning light of late afternoon.

· 27 ·

Dex stumbled, righted himself with a grab for the edge of the door jamb, and walked with a stiff gait and wooden expression to the bar at the back of the room.

"Beer," he demanded in an overly loud voice. "Want a damn beer." He fumbled in his pants pockets, first one and then the other, went back to the first and drew out a handful of small change that he promptly spilled onto the rough planking of the floor. "Shit!" he barked.

He bent low, swayed, would have toppled sideways if he hadn't reached out in the nick of time to steady himself by grasping the brass footrail.

"Shit," he repeated and began slowly, awkwardly trying to retrieve the coins he'd dropped.

A man standing nearby stooped and helped find the remaining coins. When he held them out to Dex, though, he received only a blank and glassy stare as Dex seemed not to recognize what the helpful fellow was holding or why he was offering it.

After a few moments the customer shrugged, straightened, and laid Dexter's money onto the bar surface.

The bartender gave Dex a suspicious glance as Dex grabbed hold of the bar and pulled himself upright, but he

placed a schooner of beer in front of him and extracted a
nickel from the coins the other customer had put there.

Dex belched hugely, took up his beer with both hands,
and gulped down at least half the schooner. The newly drawn
beer left a puffy wisp of white foam on Dexter's mustache.
He seemed not to notice and made no effort to wipe it away.

"Are you all right, mister?"

"Mister? Who you calling 'mister'?"

"I'm just asking if you are feeling well this evening, sir."

"I'm no plain damn 'mister'," Dex informed him, accom-
panying that information with a stern wagging of his finger
beneath the bartender's nose. "No mister. Sir's awright.
Or—" Dex belched again, his cheeks puffing out with the
force of it, and he followed that with a sly smile and a giggle.
"You c'n call me 'is Excellency."

The bartender looked pained, as if he regretted ever saying
anything in the first place.

"His Excellency," Dex went on, unnoticing, "the 'Perial
. . . scuse me . . . the *Im*perial Wizard." He hiccuped into a
fist and took in a deep breath, then burped just a little. " 'Perial Wizard. Im, dammit. Im." He coughed. "Perial." That
seemed to strike him funny, and he laughed very loudly.
When he was done laughing he gave the bartender a long,
solemn, conspiratorial look and held a finger to his lips as if
in a call for silence. "Im," he said, "perial." He looked
around, scowled darkly at the man who'd helped him recover
his dropped money, and carefully turned so that his back was
to the customer. He leaned over the bar and in a hoarse
whisper loud enough to be heard throughout the saloon said,
"Wizard."

Dex looked around as if to satisfy himself that no one was
eavesdropping and continued in the loud whisper, "D'j'you
ever meet a Perial Wizard before? No? Well you have now.
You tell that t'your grandbabies, hear? Perial damn Wizard,
'at's me. 'N some sonuvabish's fucking head gonna roll
'round here too. You know what I'm saying to you,
mister? Some-fuckin'-body gonna get his. Some-fuckin'-

body robbed me. D'j'you know tha'? They robbed me. Me. Im-fucking-perial Wizard. An' they rob me. Tha's not right, y'know. Sonuvabish gonna get his."

Dex's eyes went wide and he straightened up. Looked wildly from one side to the other, then gave the bartender an accusing glare. In a stern and authoritative voice he barked, "Tha's a secret. Don' you tell a soul. You hear me? Don' you s' much as whisper what I said. 'S all a lie anyhow. Y'know what I'm sayin'? 'S all a damn lie. Not a word of truth in it. Not one."

Dex belched, hurriedly drained what was left of his beer, and turned to wobble unsteadily away from the bar and out into the night, leaving his change forgotten on the bar.

The bartender looked at the customer who'd tried to be of help. The bartender shrugged and the customer did too.

The bartender picked up the remainder of Dex's money and dropped the coins into his apron pocket. "Care for a refill, Fred? On the house."

"Thank you, John, I expect I could enjoy one more."

John grinned. "But not as many as that fellow's had."

Fred grinned back at the bartender. "I wouldn't want to have his head come morning."

Both men laughed and returned to their evening's pursuits.

• 28 •

Dex let the outhouse door ease shut so the only sound was the creaking of the spring and not the sharp slam of wood on wood that might have wakened half the neighborhood. It was the middle of the night, and honest people should be sleeping.

That being entirely true, however, it nonetheless allowed for him to be awake at this hour, a fact which at the moment Dex found quite satisfying.

As he approached the side door to the carriage house he called out in a soft voice, "Don't get excited, James. It's only me."

"I know it is. I heard you puking your guts out in the shitter. Are you all right?" James asked from his bed in the shadows.

"Better than you think." Dex removed his coat and tie, then sat on the running board of the brougham to pull his boots off. He divested himself of the weight of the Webleys—damn but they were heavy things—and laid them on the seat of the brougham. "Did you know," he asked, "that there are eight saloons in Wharburton?"

"By actual count?" James inquired.

"By actual count," Dexter affirmed. "I know because I visited each and every one of them this evening."

"No wonder you're drunk as a lord then."

"Not hardly," Dex told him.

"But I thought—"

Dex's laugh cut the question short. "I had one beer in each place and before I got started ate half a cup of butter to coat my stomach and keep the alcohol from getting into my system."

James chuckled. "I remember that trick. Just goes to show how wrong those fools are who claim a man doesn't learn anything useful when he goes off to college."

"Yeah, well, it came in handy tonight." Dex stood and stripped off his shirt, then shucked out of his trousers.

"So tell me. If you haven't been getting drunk tonight, just what have you been doing in all eight of the saloons?"

Dexter grinned. "Planting seeds, James. I been out this evening planting some seeds. In another few days maybe we'll find out if they're going to grow. And now if you don't mind, I'm gonna get some sleep." He belched—legitimately this time—and scratched his backside. "Good night, James."

"G'night, Dex."

• 29 •

The following evening found Dexter making the rounds of the same saloons. This time he was sober. Or more accurately, this time he was willing to admit to being sober.

"Listen, uh, come closer here for a minute, will you?" He beckoned the bartender near and dropped his voice to a whisper. "Did I come in here last night?"

"You don't remember?"

Dex shook his head.

"You was here."

Dex looked to his left, then back to his right before leaning even closer to lower his voice still further. "Did I say anything that, well, that maybe I shouldn't have?"

"Mister, I been in this line o'work for seventeen years. I haven't listened to anything a customer says for at least fifteen of them years." The fellow straightened, putting a bit of distance between himself and Dex. "Do you want a beer, mister?"

Dex frowned and laid a hand on his belly. "Not again, thanks."

"Then if you don't mind, mister, I got other things to do, all right?"

"Sure. Sorry."

It was that way, or something very close to it, in all the saloons Dex visited that evening.

In all, that is, except one.

In that one the barman met him with a beer and a whiskey chaser before he had time to ask his question.

"Not tonight, thanks," Dex told him.

"It's okay, friend. On the house."

Dex lifted an eyebrow to the fellow in silent inquiry. The bartender smiled. "We like to take care of our good customers," the man said.

Dex found the comment to be of passing interest, particularly so in that he had never set foot inside the place prior to the evening before and doubly so because he hadn't bought more than a single beer in any one saloon. He'd managed to make a sloppy drunk of himself without bothering to do much in the way of actual drinking. Instead he'd been "drunk" already when he entered and only purchased the beer he did to use as a prop while he sputtered and made a spectacle of himself.

If this place regarded him today as a preferred customer, they were damn sure doing a lousy trade and should have folded long since.

Still, a drinking man can rarely be expected to turn down a free one. Dex smiled and thanked the barkeep profusely. He drank down half the whiskey and stopped at that point, not wanting to miss out on any of the flavor of what was left in the shot glass. The liquor was not the crude bar whiskey he'd fully expected but a butter-smooth and cloud-soft distillation that was as sweet on the tongue as it was in the stomach. He doubted he'd tasted anything to match it since he left home.

He cleansed his palate with a sip of the beer and then sniffed appreciatively of the whiskey before he allowed himself another taste. "This is fine," he said.

"You're a man as knows good corn, I see."

"Indeed, sir. This is a rare pleasure."

"Have another?" the barman offered.

Dex thought of their financial situation and reluctantly shook his head.

"On the house, friend."

"In that case . . ." He finished the first with pleasure and this time took note of the under-bar site where the bottle was kept. Well, not exactly a bottle. It was actually a canning jar filled with the colorless whiskey. Locally made, he gathered, and wonderfully well made at that.

"Are you a married man?" the barkeep asked.

Dex was rather taken aback by the odd question but shook his head. "Never had the pleasure. Or the curse." He smiled. "Whichever."

"Some of each, most men say."

"I, uh, assume there's a reason why you would ask that," Dex suggested.

"Sure is. A lady of my acquaintance saw you coming into the place last night," the bartender said. "She confessed to me today that she was mighty taken with you."

"Is that so?"

The barman nodded. "Naturally she couldn't come inside to get a better look."

"Naturally," Dex agreed. There were two fat whores chatting in a back corner of the saloon. But then whores don't really count when it comes to the social approbation attached to ladies socializing inside barrooms.

"She asked me to put a bug in your ear if you were to come in again, friend. I hope you don't mind."

"No, I could hardly take offense at a compliment, could I?"

"If you're interested in meeting this lady . . ." The barkeep's voice tailed off into silence.

"I would very much like to meet her," Dex told him.

The barman nodded and leaned forward. "In that case, friend, this is what you do . . ."

· 30 ·

The barkeep's instruction led Dex half a mile downriver along the Trinity and onto the grounds of the second-finest mansion he'd seen in or around Wharburton, Texas, second only to Mr. Barr's lovely home.

Perhaps because it was situated farther out along the river road this place graced a considerably larger expanse of property, the grounds consisting of cropped grass, intricate flower beds, and a handsome stand of oak and pecan trees. In a very small way the place reminded Dex of his own family's plantation manor Blackgum Bend, probably because of the pecans. For nearly as long as he could remember he'd been able to look out his bedroom window and see the familiar and comforting presence of pecan trees. He liked seeing them again here.

But then rubbernecking wasn't his purpose for coming to this house. He led himself in through the ornate iron gate across the carriage drive and followed the driveway nearly as far as the house with its lights ablaze with yellow lamplight.

Doing as the barkeep said, Dex skirted the house itself and took a flagstone footpath around to the rear where a summer kitchen sat a rod or so apart from the house.

He found the door that led into a lean-to attached to the back of the summer kitchen. There was no sound from inside, but light showed around the door frame so someone had to be inside. Dex would have thought the place a storage shed and not a residence, but who was he to know what others might choose to do? He paused only for a moment, then tapped lightly on the door.

"Who is it?"

"My name is Dexter Yancey. Carl said you invited me to stop by and, uh, make your acquaintance."

"Oh yes. One moment, please."

He heard no footsteps but within seconds the latch lifted and the door was opened to him by a slender and rather pale young woman wearing a serving girl's drab frock and frilly white apron. She even had her hair piled and pinned under a white mob cap and was the very picture of a housemaid.

She was a little bit of a thing and would have had to climb onto a stool just to look him in the eyes. She settled for peering at him, looking him up and down with obvious interest as if seeing him for the first time in her life.

"You said your name is Dexter?"

"That's right. And with whom have I the pleasure of speaking, miss?"

It took her a moment to work out what the question was. Then she quite visibly brightened and said, "My name is Annie. Come inside, Dexter."

He removed his hat, bowed slightly, and stepped across the portal into her . . . abode? Whatever.

If this was where Annie lived then she was mighty easy satisfied. And mighty little interested in surrounding herself with doodads or little niceties.

The floor was but packed earth, the ceiling unfinished, and the rough planking of the walls covered on two sides by shelving and on the other two were covered by nothing at all, nothing but raw, unsanded planks over stout framing.

The shelves, he couldn't help but notice, were bare. They held not a single item. Except, he noted, dust. And that was arranged in a pattern of circles, the circles being bare wood with dust coating the planking around them. Obviously the shelves had been used to store bottles or jars until very, very recently. Now there was no sign of anything there. Not a picture. Not a knick-knack. Nothing.

Annie's furniture consisted of a folding cot, a rocking chair, a small table, and a lamp. A can of lamp oil rested on the floor beneath the table, and there was a box of matches on it beside the lamp.

Dex could see a small, metal-braced trunk on the floor underneath the cot. The bedding consisted of a sheet, two blankets and a pillow that was not even covered with a pillowcase, exposing blue and white striped ticking.

He looked about to see what Annie might have been doing with herself when he arrived. A book. A magazine. A knitting or sewing basket. There was nothing like that anywhere in the room.

He had to force back an impulse to smile before he turned his attention to the girl.

"Carl said you saw me last night. Is that right?"

"Yes," she affirmed. "I saw you going into the Oktober Haus and I . . . I trust you will forgive me if I'm forward," she batted her eyes quite shamelessly, which Dex thought more silly than enticing, and continued, "but you are simply the most handsome and nicely set up gentleman I've ever my whole life *seen*, Mr. Yancey."

She smiled and laid a hand on his arm. "I want you to know, Mr. Yancey, that I am a decent girl. Really I am. And I've never done anything like this before. But when I saw you, why, something turned inside my heart and I knew that I simply *had* to meet you."

"You flatter me," Dex said. And that, he realized, was the truth and then some. Bald, blatant, brassy flattery was exactly what this was.

"Would you, sir," her touch left his arm and wandered up onto his cheek, "would you perhaps permit me to know you better?"

The girl's eyes were asparkle and her lips were soft and moist. She gave him the most earnest and gently yearning look he'd seen on any face since his old coon hound Lucretia Borgia passed on.

Then she lifted herself onto tiptoes, raised her elfin face to his, and—in the most shy and ladylike manner possible—began trying to suck his tongue out of his mouth and halfway down her slender and delicate little throat.

What could a gentleman do under such a circumstance? Dex allowed Annie to have her way with him.

• 31 •

Ah, Annie. A lovely and lissome little thing she was. Skinny, it was true. Her body was a collection of knobs and thinly covered bones all hung together with pale, translucent skin through which the blue traces of veins could be faintly seen.

But her tits were firm and saucy even, if somewhat less than a mouthful, and her bush was generously furred.

What the girl lacked in size she more than made up for in energy.

She wrapped herself around him arm, leg, and in between.

She sucked his tongue and repeated her efforts some distance south of there.

She climbed him like a squirrel scampering up a tree and seated herself quite happily atop the pole Dex rather thoughtfully provided for her use.

She churned her hips with such vigor that it seemed only a shame she didn't have the handle of a dasher up her butt because she could have brought butter from his cream in record time.

She bounced and wiggled, threw back her head and giggled.

Annie seemed to be quite enjoying herself.

And enthusiasm like that can only be rewarded with matching joy.

Dex gave in to the moment and let himself be used in any and every way the girl could devise.

The depths of her imagination, he soon concluded, were impressive indeed.

She had little in the way of furniture, and the folding camp cot that was her bed looked too flimsy to stand under Annie's assaults. He was sure the girl would quickly reduce the cot to a handful of canvas and splinters, but in fact she had little need for such common and mundane accessories as a bed.

She used the rocking chair, the night stand, the floor and the shelving.

She did not, thank goodness, make active use of the bedside lamp. Damn thing was, after all, burning.

But Annie's inventive nature put just about everything else in the room to excellent use, down to Dexter's quickly discarded clothing.

The girl could suck with more authority than a fire company's six-man high pressure pump, and the movement of her hips was fast and frantic enough to start that fire to begin with if only her thighs were made of dry wood . . . and if she'd allowed them to press together for more than a few seconds at a time. For the most part she kept her legs rather wide apart.

Ah, Annie. Such a delight.

At length, though, Dex had no more length to offer her. Fleshy length, that is. At least not until he had a few minutes to recuperate.

He did not think he'd ever before been so thoroughly drained, so exhaustingly sated and in so quick a time.

Sow the wind; reap the whirlwind? Annie was a whirlwind and then some. A whirlwind and a whirling dervish. She left him gasping for air.

The gasps, he would have had to admit, were achieved by drawing air past teeth that were fully exposed in a grin of purest delight.

Dex gently disengaged himself from the girl and sprawled full length onto her cot. It held his weight without protest, thank goodness, but he was so tired he wasn't sure he would have bothered to move even if the thing had collapsed under him.

"You," he said softly, "are almighty good."

Annie smiled. "Do you really think so, Mr. Yancey?"

"I'll sign an affidavit if you like."

She giggled and lay down tight against his side, her sweat mingling with his as her body pressed itself onto his.

Dex marveled at the realization that even after all that, her skin felt cool to the touch. Damp, it was true, but cool. He himself, he was sure, must have felt like a furnace. His skin was flushed, his heart was still racing from the pounding exertions and he was gulping air like a fresh-caught catfish on the river bank. Annie looked and acted like she'd scarcely begun.

"I like you," Annie said.

"And I like you, little dear," he returned.

"I want to know about you."

"Me? Oh, I'm not very interesting. Really."

"No," she insisted, "I really, *really* like you, Mr. Yancey. I want to know everything there is to know about you."

Dex kissed the girl—it fair wore him out having to turn his head the few inches necessary in order to accomplish that—and patted her tit. "Don't you think you could call me Dexter now?"

Annie giggled. Dex wasn't all that crazy about girls who were gigglers. But what the hell. Exceptions could be made to any rule. "I think I could do that, Dexter honey." She giggled. "Is that better?"

"Much better," he assured her.

"Now tell me everything about my favorite guy Dexter, please Dexter."

"What is it that you want to know, dear?"

"I told you. Everything. Who you are. Where you came from. What you are doing here. You know. Everything."

Dex smiled. He began to talk. While he talked, Annie bent over him and began to quite delicately run the tip of her pink and dainty tongue over him. Over his nipples. Into his arm-pits. Down across his belly. Into his navel. Over and around his scrotum. Onto his limp and flaccid cock.

Except, incredibly, things were not all that limp and loose down there any longer.

He wouldn't have thought it possible.

But he was not complaining and neither was Annie.

After all, they had all night to talk.

◆ 32 ◆

"Don't shoot," Dex said softly.

He faintly heard the oily, metallic double-click of a revolver hammer being lowered gently from full cock to safe and immediately thereafter James said, "Come ahead."

Dex stepped inside Mr. Barr's carriage house and dropped his hat onto the floor of the light buggy that was in the same corner where James' bed was laid out. "It isn't quite dawn yet. Didn't think you'd be awake."

"I have been, off and on, for most of the night."

"Trouble?" Dex asked.

"Lordy, I sure thought so. Couple hours after it got dark I heard some rustling and shuffling around in the leaves just the other side of this wall. I thought it was those damn Kuxers come back to finish what they started."

"Kluxers," Dex corrected.

"What?"

"Klux. They're Kluxer, not Kuxers. Damn if I know why everybody wants to call them the Ku *Kux* Klan, but they aren't. It's Ku Klux Klan. With an 'L.' Klux."

"Yes, teacher. So like I was saying, I thought it was those white-ass sons of bitches in the green hoods coming back after me again. You better believe I was glad you gave me these here pistols. Bastards might get to me again, but at least I'd have a chance to get some licks in on them first."

"I don't see any bodies laying around outside. Or did you let them retrieve their casualties?"

James chuckled, the sound furry and low in the shadows where his bed was. "Wasn't the Kux . . . excuse me . . . it wasn't the *Kluxers* after all." He bore down hard on the correct word this time. "There was a cat in season out there and at least two toms fighting over her. Damn things have kept me up most of the night."

"It sounds like you had an interesting night of it," Dex observed.

"Yeah, it was terrific. How about you?"

Dex grinned and stripped his coat off. Damn but he was tired. Worn to a nubbin. Not that he'd minded getting that way.

"I've been doing the same as those cats. Except there wasn't anybody I had to fight for the privilege."

"If it's all the same to you, white boy, I'd just as soon not hear any details. It isn't just boring and lonely lying on the ground in this shed all the time. It's making me so horny that I honk. How long has it been anyhow?"

"Hell, I dunno," Dex answered. "Twenty minutes maybe? Thirty?"

"I meant for me, idiot."

"Oh. I misunderstood."

"Sure you did. But look, I know you better than to think you brought this shit up just so you could brag that you got laid. Even a fella as ugly as you can get lucky sometimes, and I have to assume you've bedded a wench or two before tonight. What's so special about this one?"

Dex was still grinning. "It was her idea," he said. "She saw me on the street last night and was so completely infatuated that she left word with a guy where I could go to meet her."

"You're lying to me, white boy."

"No. I swear t'you, James, it's God's own truth."

"That it was love at first sight?"

Dex laughed. "Not hardly. But it's true as true can be that that lame yarn is the story I was given. With a straight face too."

"Son of a bitch must be some kind of actor if that's so," James said.

"Now I don't know why you'd react that way. I am a very handsome fellow, you know."

"In your opinion."

"And in Annie's," Dex amended.

"That's her name? Annie?"

"Uh huh. Never got around to a last name, but she calls herself Annie."

"And she fell in love with you just that quick."

"I dunno about true love, but she's certainly a lusty little bit of a thing. I can vouch for that."

"And that's all she wanted?" James asked. "To fuck?"

"That too, of course," Dex said. "And in between times she wanted to talk. Said she was so smitten with me that she wanted to know everything there was to know."

James laughed too now. "Is this where the light is supposed to dawn so that I can see how this deal takes shape?"

"I think it's reasonable for you to begin reaching conclusions now, yes."

"And you told her everything she wanted to hear?"

"Don't be silly. If I told her *every*thing, James, she wouldn't have any reason to invite me back again."

"But you planted more than one kind of seed in that little old gal, did you?"

"Aye," Dex admitted. "If you were to make that assumption, I'd not deny it."

James thought about that for a few moments. Then he sobered. "I hope you know what you're doing, Dex. These bastards aren't to be played with. Believe me."

"I won't claim that I have all the details and finer points worked out just yet. But we'll sit back and give my seeds a little time to start sprouting and see what comes up outta the ground from them. And if you don't mind now, James, I'm gonna lie down and grab a little sleep. It's been a long night."

He stepped out of his britches and climbed inside the brougham that he'd come to regard as a sort of home away from . . . any sort of comfort.

Still, it was a place to stretch out and that was all he really needed. They could worry about comfort when James was well enough to be moved.

· 33 ·

Dex moved his things into Edgar Barr's big house that day. It occurred to him that he didn't want anyone to think him overly solicitous of a lowly black servant and maybe screw up the impressions Dexter was trying to give.

Besides, James was well enough to defend himself now even if from the flat of his back. James wasn't yet mobile, but he was fully cognizant of what was going on around him now and the swelling had gone down in his face and eyes to the point that he could see normally too.

"I understand," James said when Dex explained it to him. "I'll be fine."

"If I didn't think that, you ugly black bastard, I wouldn't be leaving you here alone."

"Hell, I know that. Now you go on and do what has to be done so's we can get our licks in against these Kluxers." James grinned. "Gonna sneak up on them like a diamond-back in the grass, are you?"

Dex laughed. "With the old blind snake here," he pointed toward his fly, "leading the way."

That evening Dex took his supper with Mr. Barr, stopped in the carriage shed to make sure James was all right, and strolled down along the Trinity, arriving at Annie's barren little room an hour or so past full dark.

"I was hoping you'd come," she whispered, clinging to him in an outburst of hungry passion and exploring inside Dex's mouth with her tongue.

"I couldn't have stayed away," he told her. "Not for anything." It was a sentiment he meant more sincerely than Annie could possibly guess.

"Come inside, Dexter honey. I don't want anybody should see us in the doorway here." She giggled. "Besides, there's something I want to show you."

Annie took his hand and pulled him inside the bare little room, closing the door behind them and sliding the bolt closed.

Sometime during the day, Dex saw, Annie had taken some pains to prettify her room. Sheets, a pillowcase, and a very handsomely made patchwork quilt graced the bed now. And it was, he quickly saw, a real bed. The cot had been taken out and a sturdy brass bed substituted. There was also a rumpled and none-too-clean tapestry nailed onto one wall, softening the bleak appearance and making the place quite cozy in the light of the single lamp.

"Nice," he said.

"I thought . . ." Annie ducked her pretty head and managed a blush. "I hoped you'd like it." She giggled. "I was scared we were gonna bust that rickety ol' camp cot to kindling. You know?"

Dex laughed. "That occurred to me too, honey bunch."

Annie looked up at him past long, curling eyelashes. " 'Honey bunch.' Nobody's ever called me that before. I like it."

"And I like you, baby doll." He reached for her.

Annie did not come into his arms immediately though. She paused just long enough to give a little wiggle and a shrug of her shoulders so that her housedress slithered off and fell into an untidy heap at her feet.

She was not wearing anything beneath the thin cloth of that simple dress.

"Nice," Dex said, meaning it.

Annie giggled. And leaped into the air, wrapping her legs tight around his waist and her arms even tighter about his neck.

It was, Dex determined later, a damn good thing the new bed was stout because the cot could not possibly have withstood the excesses of the evening.

· 34 ·

Dex peered down past the flat of his belly to the limp, wet sausage nesting in his pubic hair.

"Messy," he observed. "Gonna get stains on my britches, and then everybody will know what I been up to."

Annie giggled and said, "I can take care of that, honey bunch." She slid lower on the bed until she reached the object in question, then dipped her head to it, and took him into her mouth. She swished him back and forth inside her mouth, creating a most interesting sequence of sensations. When at last she withdrew the only moisture remaining was Annie's saliva.

"You sure are tasty, honey," she said. "That's a better drink than any other I can think of."

"And one you are welcome to sample any time you wish, my dear."

"Aren't you the gallant one." She grinned and planted a wet and rather loud kiss on his belly. "D'you mind if I ask you something, Dexter?"

"You can ask me anything you like, pretty girl."

"Last night you said you're from over Looz-ianny way."

"That's right."

"You're a southern boy, right?"

"Bred and born," he agreed.

"You used to own slaves, right?"

"Of course. I told you about Blackgum Bend. You can't work a plantation without slaves." Which was an exaggeration if not exactly a lie, but it seemed a good idea under the circumstances.

"Yet they say you got you a pet nigger that you just dote on."

"Who says that?" Dex asked.

"Oh," she shrugged. "You know. Folks."

"I do have a servant with me, of course. He used to be my slave. Now, well, we both know how it is now. Let's just say this is the next best thing."

"They say you favor him. Worry about his health and like that."

"That is true enough, Annie. But then wouldn't you take care of a valuable horse if you owned one or a dog you particularly favored?"

"Sure I would," she agreed. "You like dogs?"

Dex nodded.

"I used to have a dog once. When I was little."

He laughed. "You're still little."

Annie made a face, then giggled. "You know what I mean. When I was young."

"Tell me about your dog, Annie."

She did. By the time she was done she was crying. "I never found out what happened to him. My papa carried him off and I never seen him again. He was a sweet dog, too. I miss him. It's been, gee, five years now. An' I still miss him."

Dex petted the back of her head. The dog might have been a sweet pup, but Annie for sure was a sweet girl, he thought. Never mind the fact that she was being paid to spy on him. He quite honestly liked her.

Which was not to say that he trusted her. Not hardly. But he did genuinely like her.

"May I tell you something, Annie dear?"

"You can tell me anything you want, Dexter." She dried her tears with the knuckles of her hand, leaving her eyes red and moist.

"Annie, my little honey bunch, I think you are probably the prettiest, the sweetest, and the dearest little liar I have ever in my life known."

She blinked and jerked upright into a sitting position beside him on the bed. "Why'd you go and say an awful thing like that, Dexter?"

"That you are pretty and sweet and dear? I said those things because they are all true."

"No, I mean . . . you know. About me lying? Dex honey, I wouldn't lie to you."

He took her hand, drew it to his lips, and very tenderly kissed her palm, each of her fingertips, and finally the back of her hand. "Shall we say then, dear, that you have not been totally forthcoming in our conversations?"

"I don't know what you mean by that, sweetie."

"Of course you do, Annie. And please understand, dear. I don't fault you for it. I'm not angry." He smiled. "On the contrary, little love, I am delighted that circumstance brought us together. In fact, I hope I will be permitted to see more of you. But I am not a stupid man nor vain enough to think that one look at me would send a girl so lovely and fine as you into throes of passion. Why, Annie my sweet, you could have any man in Wharburton, Texas, or for fifty miles in any direction. You are far and away the prettiest girl I've seen since the last time I was in New Orleans."

It was Dex's experience that when it comes to flattery, it is damn near impossible for a gentleman to gild the lily overmuch.

Annie preened and giggled and practically quivered with delight at the compliments. "Do you mean that, Dexter? D'you *really* think I'm as pretty as the fine ladies in N'Orleans?"

"I mean it most sincerely, Annie. There's scarcely a one of those ladies who could hold a candle to light your beauty."

"You're fibbing, Dexter Yancey." She sounded most willing to have the accusation refuted.

"I swear it." Dex made a spitting sound onto the tip of his forefinger and used the digit to cross his heart with an imaginary X.

"You bein' from Looz-iana, I guess you would know about those things," Annie said.

"I would. I've spent many a happy week in New Orleans, dear, and admired many a shapely ankle. I can tell you in all sincerity that you outshine even those gracious and lovely creatures."

"Gosh, I wish I could believe you, honey."

"You can." He sat up and leaned forward to give her a gentle kiss. "I want you to believe and to understand too, sweet Annie, that I have no ill will for you. You've done what you were asked. What someone, I don't know who and I don't know why, what they required to be done. That is fine, Annie. I really don't mind that in the slightest." He paused, considering, then decided that if it was impossible to overstate that sort of thing, why the hell not go all the way with it. "If they'd sent someone with less class and beauty I might not have caught on, Annie dear, but you aren't the sort of girl who ever needs to seek out a gentleman. One look and the eligible boys will all be swarming around you."

"But Dexter, honest, I—"

He placed a finger over her lips. "Shush now, Annie dear. It's all right. Truly I don't mind. Just ask me openly and honestly the things they want you to learn from me. I promise to answer every question you put to me just as completely as I know how. And then after we're done talking, Annie my precious little honeybee, I want to take you into my arms again and know the joy of you."

"Dexter, you make me feel so ashamed." She bent her head and began to weep.

"That was not my object, sweet Annie. I want to assure you that I don't mind your questions. Really I don't. I'm just happy that they brought me together with you like this." He pulled her to him, holding her close and repeatedly hugging and kissing and cuddling her.

Eventually Annie became calm again and even seemed to accept Dexter's assurances.

They talked after that. For quite a while. And when the talking was done, Annie blew out the lamp flame and they made love in a slow and gentle cadence that hadn't been present in their earlier couplings.

The girl was actually falling for him, Dex realized, and then, having made her feel the shame of her mission, he himself felt a taste of it for using Annie in turn.

Still, it was something that had to be done and if the girl suffered because of it, well, he would simply have to bear that responsibility.

• 35 •

"C'mon, Dex. You're a big boy now. You know how things are. The girl is a whore. Whores lie. Nothing personal about this one, mind. It's just their nature to lie. You can't go pinning our future onto something you heard from a whore."

"You weren't there, James. This girl was telling the truth. Well, about some things. And I'm not 'pinning' anything on her word, dammit. I'm just . . . getting ideas. You know?"

"I know that you can't count on anything she said, Dex. She will have told you whatever she was paid to tell you and she'll have learned from you whatever she was paid to learn."

"Up to a point," Dex said. "But past that . . ." He shrugged. "I could see it in her eyes, James. I could feel it in her flesh."

"Oh, I can believe you felt of her flesh, all right. But truth, honesty, and the Christian ethic ain't exactly what I'd expect you to find there."

"Have I ever mentioned to you how unbecoming sarcasm is?"

"In a nigger?" James snapped.

"In a friend," Dex shot back at him, scowling.

"I . . ." James turned his head and stared at the blank side wall of the carriage house. Dex thought he looked close to tears. "Shit, Dex, I'm sorry. That was cheap, wasn't it."

"Yeah, it was, and I don't think I deserved it."

"I know you didn't. I'm just—"

"Frustrated as hell," Dex finished for him.

James nodded.

"Tired of hurting every time you try to roll over."

"Yeah."

"Weary to death of needing me to help you just so you can take a shit or pee without wetting yourself."

"You got that right."

"You wish to hell you could jump up and do something to help."

"Of course."

Dex hunkered down close beside the pallet where James spent his days and nights. He touched his friend's shoulder and said, "The biggest help you can give right now is to get your black ass healthy and able to travel again. If I do figure out a way to slide in like a diamondback and strike these sons of bitches, I'll need you ready to get the hell outta here with me. Besides," his voice may have thickened just a little, "besides, damn you, I'd miss you if anything serious happened to you. You're an ugly bastard and wouldn't bring much on an auction block, but I'm used to having you around. I expect I'd just as soon keep you with me as not. You know it?"

"I know it, Dex. I apologize. I just . . . got to feeling sorry for myself for a minute there. I'll get over it."

"Good, because I might need your help if we're gonna make out with teaching these Texas boys not to fuck around with a couple coon-ass Cajuns."

James looked up at Dexter. And began to laugh in spite of the pain the jostling caused him. "Cajuns. Us! Jesus, Dex, you're as much a coon-ass as I am, and you know those Cajun boys down south would hang my black butt from a high oak tree if I claimed there was anything coon-ass or Cajun about me."

Dex grinned at his friend. "See. You look an' sound more like your old self already."

"Dickhead," James accused.

"Dumbfuck," Dex returned.

The two old friends grinned at each other for a moment. Then, the fleeting moment ended, Dex stood, his knee joints popping. "Go to sleep, James. What d'you want I should bring you out for breakfast?"

"Crêpes suzette," James mused, rolling his eyes. "Cherries jubilee. And a cute little ol' black girl to take care of my, uh, problem."

"How about you settle for the crêpe?" Dex suggested. "I'll bring you a nice, hot one. You can wrap it around your problem and—"

"Jesus, Dex, don't make me laugh, okay?"

"G'night, James."

"Good night your own self, Dexter."

Dex felt pretty good, everything considered, as he ambled through the garden toward the guest room he'd been given in Mr. Barr's elegant home.

◆ 36 ◆

Dexter rather expected to have visitors the next day, but he did not. Instead he was approached by a rather shy and diffident Mrs. Collum when Dex was on his way to join Mr. Barr in the old gentleman's study before dinner.

"I might've done something bad today, Mr. Yancey. I might owe you an apology, sir."

"How's that, Mrs. Collum?"

"Well I was at the store this afternoon. Like always. Buying a piece of meat for dinner tonight. You know?"

Dex didn't know or particularly care, but he nodded and waited for the lady to go on with whatever this was about.

"I saw Mrs. Overton there."

Mrs. Collum acted as if that was supposed to mean something. Dex had no idea what.

"Mrs. Overton spoke to me. She's never done anything like that before, her being a proper lady you understand and me just being a widow woman and a housekeeper."

Dex muttered something that Mrs. Collum was welcome to take however she wished, as sympathy or understanding, commiseration or whatever.

"Mrs. Overton was asking about you, Mr. Yancey. And I never thought. I just, well, I told her whatever she asked.

About you, I mean. Your family and all. Not that I know so
awful much, but naturally Mr. Barr has spoken about you
from time to time lately and about your father for as long as
I've known him. Mr. Barr was terribly fond of your father,
you know."

"As my father was of him also," Dex agreed.

"Yes, sir. Well like I was saying, Mrs. Overton asked me
these questions about you, and I . . . I suppose I was so startled to be talking to someone like her that I just rattled right
on. Told her everything I knew, not that it's so much. But
then . . . later, I mean . . . then I got to thinking when I was
on my way home how you might not want anyone knowing
about your private self, sir, and I thought . . . I thought I'd
best talk to you now and tell you what I did and, well, apologize to you, sir, if I've done something to upset or offend
you."

Dex smiled and assured the woman, "Mrs. Collum, I have
no objection to you telling anyone anything that is true."

Mrs. Collum looked positively aghast. "Oh, sir! I wouldn't
make things up about you. I would never do anything like
that."

Dex laughed and told her, "Of course not, and I didn't
mean to imply otherwise. Just please understand that I do
not mind your conversation in the slightest and take no offense whatsoever. May I ask you one thing though?"

"Yes of course, sir, anything."

"What meat did you find for us tonight?" He realized as
he said it that he really did need to contribute something to
the household larder. He and James had little in their pockets,
but it seemed that Mr. Barr's circumstances were even worse
and Dex did not want to be a burden on the gentleman.

"A ham, sir," Mrs. Collum was saying. "A very nice one,
I think. I hope you will like it."

"Judging from everything I've had of your cooking so far,
Mrs. Collum, I have no doubt that this will be a meal to
remember with great fondness. You are quite a fine cook, if
you don't mind me saying so."

The housekeeper ducked her eyes and blushed just a little, quite obviously pleased with the compliment.

Later—and the meal did prove to be excellent, as he'd fully expected—he took James' supper out to the carriage house and told James about the brief chat with Mrs. Collum.

"Sounds like your prey is starting to sniff at the bait, doesn't it?" James observed.

"So it would appear," Dex agreed.

"What now?"

"Wait," he said without hesitation. "We let them make the next move." Dex smiled. "I wouldn't want to seem overeager now would I?"

"And the girl?"

"Oh, I have to keep on seeing her, of course. After all, I've become smitten with her, right? But I've also let them know that I'm onto the game. They're bound to want to know now how much I'm onto and how much of what I told Annie is true. Seems only reasonable they'd try to verify what I've said before they accept any of it."

"You think they'll come around here to ask me anything?" James reached under the quilt that lay in his lap. That was where his revolvers were hidden.

"Until they decide one way or the other what they should think about me," Dex said, "I think you're as safe as if I had you locked inside the vault over at the Wharburton bank."

"But if somebody does come?"

"Don't take any chances, James. If somebody walks in here, you do whatever you have to to defend yourself."

"And if it's just some poor son of a bitch come to grease a buggy axle?"

Dex shrugged. "First you blow his nuts off. You can apologize after if it turns out you were wrong to do it."

"I'll tell him you said so."

"You do that."

"Are you gonna help me to sit up so I can feed myself without dribbling everything?" James asked.

"Feeling cocky tonight, are you? You want to sit up to eat? And feed yourself, too?"

"It's hard to keep a good man down," James said.

"How the hell would you know?" Dex asked as he began gathering seat cushions and an old wicker picnic hamper that he thought he could pile behind James as a backrest. This was good progress, he thought. Excellent.

◆ 37 ◆

"Dexter, honey."

"Yes, sweetheart?" He picked her up and kissed her thoroughly. She felt like she weighed scarcely more than a good sized housecat, but small size did not mean she was lacking in anything else. She kissed him back with fervor and wriggled with pleasure when she felt Dex's response.

"I have a favor to ask," she murmured, her lips still pressing lightly against his.

"Anything," he said.

"I want you to come someplace with me," Annie said.

"I intend to come someplace *in* you. Will that do?"

"I'll take care of that first, honey. But will you do that for me? Please?"

Dex lowered her to the floor and raised an eyebrow.

"What's this about, Annie?" He rather suspected that he already knew. But he did not want to let on to her that he did.

"It's my boss, Dex. I hope you don't mind. I was talking to him about you. You know. What a sweet fella you are and like that. I didn't say nothing that I shouldn't have, so I hope you ain't mad."

"I'm not mad," he assured her, meaning it.

"Yeah, well anyway, I was telling my boss about you, and he said he'd like to meet you and one thing kinda led to another and I sort of promised him that I'd bring you by tonight to meet him and some of his gentleman friends."

"You want me to go meet a bunch of strangers?"

"If you'd do that for me, Dexter, I'd appreciate it *ever* so much. I really would." She smiled and lightly stroked the bulge below his belt that threatened to pop the buttons off his fly. "Right now, honey, an' again when you're done visiting with Harry. With Mr. Carter, that is. Harry Carter. He's the gentleman I work for. The one I was telling about you."

This was going along just fine, Dex thought. Aloud, he said, "You want me to go over to the house and meet this man you work for?" He inclined his head in the direction of the mansion behind which Annie's makeshift quarters were situated.

"Not right away, honey. I'll take care of this for you first off." She petted him again and began unfastening the strained buttons even before she dropped onto her knees. "Then we'll walk over to this place where Mr. Carter and his friends will be. Don't worry. It isn't far. Then later on when you're done talking with him and his gentlemen friends, why, you can come back here an' you and me can snuggle up and do whatever it is you want, honey. Anything, sweetie. Anything at all that you want, I'll be there to do it for you. Okay?"

"Sure, Annie. Whatever you say, baby." Dex closed his eyes and almost lost his balance. He had to reach out and lean against the door jamb to steady himself as wave after wave of exquisite sensation flooded through him. Annie's mouth was sweet and wet and hot, and she engulfed him gently, drawing him deep and then receding to allow cool air to touch wet and rigid flesh each time she withdrew.

"Whatever you say," Dex mumbled again as he concentrated all his attention on what the girl was doing now.

• 38 •

Annie took him not to the back door of the mansion as he'd expected but further down along the bank of the river to a small and rickety cabin that looked like it would belong not to a wealthy man but to a sharecropper or the lowest sort of common laborer.

It was too dark for him to make out much in the way of details, of course, especially since the cabin was set deep inside a copse of mixed oak and softwoods. Which, when he thought about it, made very little sense. Any place put up as a dwelling would normally be situated in a clearing—if not right away then certainly as soon as the land could be cleared—to allow for a garden plot, outbuildings, wood storage, and the like.

This place was isolated and largely hidden from view.

Annie seemed more than a little nervous when they approached the place. The hand that clutched Dexter's was moist and clammy, and her pace dragged slower and slower the closer they got.

"Are you all right?" Dex asked as the girl paused at the steps to take a deep breath and steel herself before stepping onto the porch and tapping sharply on a door that was surrounded by a thin halo of yellow lamplight.

"Mr. Carter, sir? It's me. Annie. I'm here with Mr. Yancey, sir, like you said."

There was a moment's hesitation, then the sound of footsteps on the floorboards inside.

The door was opened not by Annie's Mr. Carter but by a man already familiar to Dex.

"Good evening, Deputy."

Barney Garrison ignored Dex for the moment to peer down at Annie from his great height. He scowled at her and jerked his thumb in the general direction of the darkness. "Get lost, bitch."

Dexter smiled, touched the brim of his hat to the deputy, and took Annie by the elbow as she went pale and turned hurriedly away.

"Where are you going, mister?"

"With the young lady, of course. I would hardly expect her to walk alone through these woods at night, could I?"

"I thought you were here to see Mr. Carter."

"So did I," Dex said. "Give the gentleman my regrets, please." He touched his brim again and led Annie to the edge of the porch.

"Wait." It wasn't Deputy Garrison's voice. Dex turned back to see Garrison replaced in the open doorway by a tall, slender gentleman in a cutaway coat and gaiters.

The gentleman bowed slightly to Annie and said, "Would you mind returning home to wait for your friend, miss? If you're uncomfortable about walking alone, I know the good deputy would be pleased to see you safely back to your own place."

Annie looked to be quite thoroughly frightened by that suggestion although she'd exhibited no fear a moment earlier at the prospect of walking alone in the dark. "As you say, sir. Dexter honey, I'll be fine. You come back whenever you're done, hear?" She looked at Carter—or so Dex assumed the gentleman to be—and dropped into a hasty curtsy, bobbing her head and gathering up her skirts to hurry down the steps and flee into the night.

Dex looked after her for a moment. He gathered the girl had no desire to be alone in the woods with Deputy Garrison. Dex found that interesting.

But not something he should be thinking about right now.

He sketched a broad and cheerful smile onto his lips and turned back to face Carter with his right hand extended. "Dexter Lee Yancey of Blackgum Bend Plantation, sir." Never mind that that was no longer current and correct. It was close enough for this son of a bitch's purposes. Dex's smile grew even bigger as his hand clasped Carter's in a gush of friendship and good will. "At your service, sir."

• 39 •

"I thought there would be more of you," Dex said casually as he walked into the middle of the one-room cabin and surveyed the scene as if he were a prospective buyer thinking about whether to make an offer.

There were four men there, including Carter and Garrison. The other pair were seated at a card table, although there were no cards in evidence, only a whiskey bottle and some small glasses.

"More of . . . you don't even know who we are," Carter blurted. "Didn't Annie tell you you'd be meeting her boss?"

"Of course she did," Dex told him. "But you hired her for this occasion. She isn't your maid."

"Did she—"

Dex waved the question away. "She didn't have to explain the details. I was expecting this. Why do you think I pretended to be drunk the other night?"

"But you . . . you don't even know who we are. Except for a few names, that is."

Dex gave the man a pitying look, as one would to a child who is particularly slow to learn a lesson taught. "You are the leaders of the Ku Klux Klan in this vicinity. At least I certainly hope you are. I've gone to a lot of bother for nothing if you aren't." He smiled and amended that. "Not that all of it was a waste of time, mind you. The girl is very good."

"But if you—"

Dex ignored him. "Sit down, please. Both of you. Thank you." He found another chair against a side wall and dragged it to the table, helping himself to a seat without waiting for invitation, then waved away the offer of a glass that one of the men held out toward him.

"Now," Dex said with no trace of doubt or hesitation in his demeanor, "I believe you gentlemen have something that belongs to me. More accurately, you have something that belongs to the Order. I will thank you to return it now, if you please."

"We don't know what you—"

Dex's expression hardened and turned cold. "Do not lie to me and do not try to cheat the Knights of the Order," he said in a low but steely tone. "Is the money here?"

"It is not," Carter said.

"You know where I am staying."

"Yes, of course, but—"

"Have the money returned to me tomorrow forenoon." He looked at Garrison. "You may bring it."

"Yes, sir," Garrison responded quickly, then looked amazed to have heard his own response. He gave Carter a sheepish glance as if to assure himself that he'd done the right thing.

"You can't waltz in here and begin issuing orders like this," Harry Carter protested. "We don't even know who you are or what you want with us. We don't know—"

"You don't know very much," Dex interjected, again cutting the man off before he could finish speaking, "and you'll know nothing at all unless I decide to include this chapter in the revival of the Order throughout our glorious southland and on into the western states and the Mid-west, will you. No, don't bother to answer that. It is true whether you know it or not. The decision will be mine and mine alone. If I turn you away there will be no appeal and no reconsideration. I will determine if you are fit to remain true Knights.

"Now. First I want to know about each of you four. Who you are, which offices you hold, what your goals and ideals are. I want to know everything. Hold nothing back, but I warn you. Do not attempt to embellish. I want all of the truth and only the truth. Have I made myself clear about this, gentlemen?"

Harry Carter looked quite unhappy, the other three quite confused.

This was not at all what they'd come here to see and hear and do.

"You," Dex said, stabbing a forefinger in the direction of Barney Garrison's wide eyes. "You will begin."

"Yes, sir," Garrison said meekly. "You already know my name and my occupation. As for my job, sir, I'm Sergeant of Arms and Tiler for the Wharburton Chapter, sir, and I—"

Garrison rattled on at length—more, actually, than Dex was particularly interested in learning. By the time he was finished the others had passively accepted the idea that Dexter Yancey—His Excellence the Imperial Wizard, that is—was present and very much in charge.

· 40 ·

"The good news," Dex said, "is that these sons of bitches won't be bothering you any more. The bad news is that I have no idea what the fuck it is these people are up to."

"I thought you said they told you everything," James said. It was shortly after dawn the following morning, and Dex had carried a tray out to the carriage house and propped James up so he could eat while they talked. "And next time, by the way, I'd appreciate it if you'd bring me something with some flavor to it. I'm getting kinda tired of grits and gravy and porridge with milk and sugar on it. I want something I can put my teeth into and chew on."

"You're feeling better this morning."

"Especially now that you say these Kluxers won't be coming after me any more. You sure about that, white boy?"

"As sure as I've got them flummoxed."

"Which is another question, isn't it?"

"You doubt the powers of the Imperial Wizard, do you?"

"Jeez, don't say that. I've had about enough of those offay bastards in the green hoods."

"White," Dex corrected.

"Pardon me?"

"White hoods. From now on they're to wear white hoods. No more green."

"Why is that?"

Dex grinned. "Keep a man busy following orders and it's not so likely he'll stop and take time to wonder why he's having to do this bullshit. Or just who it is that's issuing the orders."

"You told them to change the color of their hoods? Just like that?"

"Sure," Dex said with a laugh. "I told them it's a symbol of the new Klan."

James laughed too. Then began to cough. He shook his head and after a moment was able to say, "Lordy, don't get me to laughing, Dex. My chest and belly are still too sore to stand much of that. But no shit, you really told them that? And they *bought* it?"

"It seemed a good enough idea at the time," Dex said happily.

"What else did you tell them?"

"A bunch of bullshit. Mostly I didn't tell them; I just gave orders. More crap like the hoods."

"And you really think you have them fooled into thinking you're this Imperial fucking Wizard or something," James said.

"Damn right, I do. Hell, James, I've even made them change the grand hailing sign and the secret passwords and handshake."

"Why'd you do that?"

"Because, you idiot, I never knew what the original signs were. I mean, I knew there was such a thing. My asshole brother was a Kluxer, you know. He used to dress up in his regalia and parade around like a rooster with a hard-on. I would have joined the Klan myself if it hadn't been for Louis being made an officer. I didn't want to be associated with any bunch of people that would include him, much less elect him to something." Dexter's younger twin Louis—fraternal twin, he was careful to point out whenever the subject arose—was not among his favorite people.

"Hell, Dex, I'd have joined the Klan myself except for this one little drawback," James said and went into another spasm of unwanted coughing.

"You liked him, too," Dex said when James' coughing subsided. He didn't have to specify who he meant by the remark.

"You know I did. He was one of the finest gentleman I ever met, and you know it. No, I take that back. He was *the* finest gentleman I've met. And you felt the same way about him. I know good and well that you did."

Dex nodded. They'd both admired General Nathan Bedford Forrest almost to the point of deifying him. Forrest had visited Blackgum Bend on five separate occasions after the war, the first time simply as a courtesy so he could personally thank Dexter's father Charles Yancey for his help during the war.

During the Tennessee campaigns, after Forrest had had his famous falling out with Braxton Bragg, the general was relieved of command, stripped of his troops, and sent into what the vindictive and none-too-bright Bragg fully intended to be the backwaters of conflict.

Forrest, whose genius in warfare was exceeded only by his determination, refused to be cast aside. Instead he raised, armed, and equipped his own body of troops and returned to the fray.

Charles Yancey had been instrumental in providing the arms and equipment Forrest needed then, not only supplying money for the armaments but taking personal charge of a smuggling operation necessary to get some of the equipment past the Federals who occupied New Orleans at the time.

After the war Forrest called on Blackgum Bend to express his appreciation for Charles Yancey's support. He returned several times afterward out of friendship for the Yancey family, stopping at the Blackgum Bend landing when he traveled the Mississippi River. The general and Dexter's father had gotten along well, and General Forrest was always a more than welcome guest at the Yancey plantation.

Dex was only a child the first time he met the general but was in his teens the next time the man came and—he tried to think back—already in his twenties, he thought, the last time General Forrest was a guest of the Yanceys. James, of course, was a year younger. Both had been old enough to be awed by the general's intelligence, his kindness, and by a thoroughly natural and unfeigned courtly manner.

"He didn't look down on me," James said wistfully. "I think he's about the only white man—next to you, if anybody'd want to consider you a grown man—that looked at me like he expected I could have a brain in my head. Like I wasn't just some watermelon-eatin' field nigger but a real human person."

"He was a fine man. The south—no, the *nation*—lost a real treasure when the general died."

"And now these sons of bitches here are making something dirty of the organization that General Forrest started," James said.

"They're damn sure trying to," Dex agreed. "But maybe we can poke a stick into their spokes. What do you think?"

"I think I'd like some more of this coffee if you wouldn't mind pouring it for me, white boy."

Dex got the coffee and stirred in cream and extra sugar. James needed all the energy he could get, he figured.

They heard footsteps on the garden path and a moment later Mrs. Collum tapped on the door before peeking in. "Deputy Garrison has come to call on you, Mr. Yancey. What shall I tell him, sir?"

Dex winked at James and gave his friend a quick grin that the housekeeper could not see. "No need to carry a message, Mrs. Collum. I'll come see what he wants myself, thank you."

Mrs. Collum withdrew, and Dex gave James a thumbs-up before he followed her back to Mr. Barr's house.

If he indeed had the local chapter of the Ku Klux Klan hoodwinked—an unusually appropriate term for the occasion, Dex thought—then this would be the proof of the pudding, for they were not likely to turn over a thousand dollars of ill-gotten gains to just any jackanapes wandering in off the street.

· 41 ·

Deputy Garrison was waiting in Mr. Barr's study. Alone, Dex noted. There was no sign of Mr. Barr as common courtesy would ordinarily require it as Garrison was there to see a guest in the home and not Mr. Barr himself.

Dex knew Mr. Barr was awake and dressed. They'd shared a breakfast table not half an hour earlier. Still, his host's manners were not Dexter's responsibility. He greeted the big deputy without any display of enthusiasm. After all, Garrison was a mere underling while Dex was the Grand Imperial Wizard, having decided in his night thoughts to add a "Grand" to his assumed title of Imperial Wizard. It just seemed . . . tidier, he thought. More impressive to the *hoi polloi, eh wot*?

"Garrison." He nodded, trying to look sage and disinterested in spite of the importance of the deputy's actions this morning as a gauge of Dex's standing with the Wharburton KKK.

"Good morning, sir."

"You have something for me, I believe."

"Yes, sir, I . . ." Garrison arched his neck and cleared his throat. He looked uncomfortable. "Sir. I, um, officially I must tell you that an anonymous informer last night gave me information that led to the recovery of certain, ahem, properties which I believe may have been stolen from an, uh, from a person employed by you."

It was a long way around things, but Dex understood quite good and well what was going on here. Garrison was covering his own ass. In the unlikely event that Garrison's boss or perhaps the parish—county it was here in Texas, he had to remind himself—in the event some officer of the county ever inquired, Garrison wanted to create the fiction that Dex's money was stolen by party or parties unknown and was recovered by way of this nonexistent tipster. That was fine by Dex. No harm done whatsoever.

Dex bowed his head a fraction of an inch in mute appreciation of the circumlocution. "That is very good police work, Deputy. I commend you."

"Thank you, sir. And now if you could identify the, uh, material that was recovered?"

Garrison reached into a leather folio he'd brought with him and from it brought out the money belt. With no apparent qualm he handed it over.

The belt felt quite satisfyingly heavy. "Thank you, deputy. Have you counted the contents?"

"Yes, sir, of course. There are coins and currency . . . mostly currency . . . in the amount of eight hundred seventy eight dollars."

"Really," Dex said. "There should have been eleven hundred twenty-something."

Garrison looked stricken. His eyes bulged and his mouth dropped open. "Sir, I . . . I don't know what to say. I thought . . . that is . . . sir, I really thought it was all there."

That statement quite obviously was not part of the sham script Garrison had been reciting from moments earlier. The big man really had thought the contents of the money belt were intact.

Dex kept his expression cold and imperious. "More than eleven hundred, Deputy," he said. In fact he had no idea what the true figure should have been. But he was pretty sure it was more than a thousand. Hell, it could have been eleven something.

Garrison looked distinctly uncomfortable. "I don't know what to tell you, sir."

"I suggest you find your anonymous informer," Dex said, his tone making it clear that the so-called suggestion was in fact very much an instruction. "And I suggest you mention this to certain other parties you and I both know. I expect a full report back on this matter, Deputy. Today."

"Sir, I . . . I don't know if that will be possible. Really I—"

"Today," Dex said brusquely. He tipped his head back a bit so he could glare down the length of his nose at the uncomfortable and fidgeting deputy sheriff who was half a head taller and half a hundredweight heftier than Dexter. "Today," he repeated in a voice that was menacingly soft.

Dex unceremoniously threw the weighty money belt back at Garrison. The article struck the deputy in his more than ample belly, and he had to clutch at it awkwardly to keep it from falling to the floor. While Garrison was occupied with the money belt Dex disdainfully turned his back on the big man and stalked out of old Mr. Barr's study.

• 42 •

"My God, Dex. You had the money right there in your hands and you *gave it back*?" James groaned, rolling his eyes and shaking his head at the same time. "You should have grabbed it while you had it. We could've gotten the hell out of here."

"You aren't fit to travel yet."

"Try me. Get our money back, hire a spring wagon, and try me, why don't you?" James countered.

"One good reason is that I want more from those sons of bitches than to get our money back. I want the ass of whoever it was that did this to you."

"Look. Dexter. I don't know how to tell you this, but I'm nothing but a broad back and a weak mind. Nothing but a worthless ol' black boy. You know?"

"You're a hell of a lot more than that to me."

"That's to you. I'm talking about the world. You know. The real one? It's right out there, Dexter." He pointed toward the carriage house wall and far, far beyond it. "It's big and it's ugly and it don't give a good God damn about po' niggers. Or for that matter about smartass white boys who don't know when to cut their losses, take what they can get, and run like hell."

"We'll go when we have our money, James. And our satisfaction."

"I still think you should've kept hold of what you had in your hand while you had it. Whyever did you give it back to him?"

"Because it wasn't all there, of course. Besides, what is the first rule you have to keep in mind when you're handling an ornery son of a bitch of a stud horse?"

James thought for a moment. "Let somebody else do it?"

"Not a bad rule," Dex conceded, "but that isn't exactly what I had in mind. The rule I meant is that you never want that SOB to get it into his head that he can win. You never let him know that he's bigger than you or that he's stronger than you or that he has a prayer of beating you. Never mind that he could kick the shit out of you any time he wanted to. You never let him know that. You dominate him and make him do what you damn well want him to no matter what he tries. Right?"

"I'd still rather hire somebody else to do that shit," James insisted.

"Fine. But these Wharburton KKKers aren't stud horses and—"

"So why'd you bring horses into this anyway?" James interrupted.

"Will you let me finish, please?"

"Sorry, massa," James said with no hint of contrition in either voice or facial expression.

"My point," Dex said, "is that these people have to believe that I'm the one in control here. As long as they believe it, it's true. Remember that."

"Yessuh, massa."

Dex gave James a look of disgust but did not bother fussing at him. That would only have encouraged him anyway, and Dex knew it.

"They'll come up with the missing money. I'm counting on it. How much was supposed to be in that belt anyway?" he asked.

"Eight hundred and something," James responded. Then, a moment later, he laughed at Dex's suddenly baleful look and said, "No, actually it was something over a thousand. Not quite eleven hundred, I think. I'm not sure exactly what the amount was, but I know it was over a thousand."

"It's going to be interesting to see just how contrite and helpful these boys prove to be, isn't it?"

"Yeah, but it would o' been a whole lot simpler to take the eight hundred and run. I'm telling you, Dex, you've practically gone down on your knees and asked for trouble by stringing this out for the last damn penny."

"Penny, my ass," Dex said. "I'd pay the whole eleven hundred, or whatever the hell it was, to get a crack at the boys that roughed you up. We aren't going to let anybody get away with that, dammit. Not hardly."

"Sometimes, Dexter, I wish you was black. You'd have a more reasonable attitude if you were. More accommodating and less choosy when it comes to what you expect out of life. You know?"

"Go to sleep, James. Get to feeling better. My boots need fresh blacking and you're lying there on your ass instead of fetching and carrying for me. Get better, dammit, so you can do for me properly."

James snorted. "That'll be the day. I'll get better, all right, but it won't be so I can fetch and carry for the likes of you, boy. More so I can whip your pale and scrawny ass."

"In your dreams, bud. Only in your dreams."

James' expression became serious again. "Dex."

"Yeah, guy?"

"Get our money back, any of it you can get hold of, and let's get out of here. Okay? I got to tell you, I don't much care for this town."

"Soon," Dex promised. "We'll do what we got to do, then we'll be gone really soon."

"I hope to hell you're right about that," James told him.

· 43 ·

The messenger came that evening while Dex and Mr. Barr were at supper. Mrs. Collum appeared at Dex's elbow and in a low voice announced, "There is a man outside on the porch to see you, Mr. Yancey."

Dex took his cue from the housekeeper and excused himself from the table. Better to receive the fellow outside than to ask Mrs. Collumn to show him in given the wording she'd chosen to use.

When he saw the visitor Dex understood Mrs. Collum's reluctance to have the man come into the Barr home as a guest. The fellow was a rather poor specimen of humanity. He had yellow teeth, unkempt hair, and broken fingernails.

He also, however, had impeccable credentials to submit. He greeted Dex with a nervous bob of his head and then, the tip of his tongue showing at the corner of his mouth as he concentrated on remembering, he offered up the correct secret handshake of the Ku Klux Klan and the secret sign as well, to which Dex responded with the correct secret countersign. Dex knew that all were correct because he himself had invented them not twenty four hours earlier. Obviously this poor fellow had been laboring during the day to memorize the new order of things.

"What's your name, son?" Dex asked in a wise and fatherly tone, never mind that the messenger was probably a dozen years older than he.

"Robert, sir. Your excellence. Sir. Robert Hapes."

"I take it you have something to tell me, Robert?"

"Yes, sir. Grand Dragon Carter says I should tell you there will be a gathering of the Klavern tonight soon after full dark. You can meet him at his house, sir. At your convenience. He said I was t'remember to tell you that part. We'll gather soon as it's convenient for you. Sir."

"Thank you, Robert. Is there anything else?"

Dex was rather hoping there would be assurances sent regarding the money, but Robert Hapes only shook his head and said, "Nothing else, sir. Just what I already tol' you."

"Very well, Robert. You may inform the Grand Dragon that I shall join him later this evening."

"Yes, sir. Thank you, sir." Hapes bobbed his head and stepped backward several paces, still bobbing and bowing, before he turned and scurried down the porch steps and away.

Dex stood for several moments pensively watching the man go, then turned and went back to his supper.

There was no light showing inside the lean-to where Annie had been. Dex went there first, thinking to enjoy a little companionship—or something—before meeting with Carter and the Klan, but Annie was not there. Neither was any of the furniture she'd been using there. Dex tried the door, thinking she might be inside. The door was latched but not locked and opened freely to him. There was no sign of the few things that had been brought in to make the shed seem a sleeping room, and now the shelves were laden with jars of pickles and jams and whatever else Carter stored here as the flare of a sulphur match disclosed.

Dex was disappointed. He'd been looking forward to another tryst with the girl. He was not, however, all that surprised. The idea of Annie as a serving girl smitten with instant desire had been a little hard to swallow from the outset, and Dex found that he was able now to accept a dose of truth without doing any serious hurt to his sense of self-worth or well-being.

Instead he turned back the way he'd just come and made his way around to the front door of the Carter mansion.

A Grand Imperial Wizard should not, after all, have to present himself at the servants' entrance.

• 44 •

The Grand Dragon, replete in hood and flowing white robes and an impressively weighty brass ornament hung around his neck, led the somewhat less grandly attired Grand Imperial Wizard past the cabin where they'd met the previous night and along a path further down the Trinity to what appeared to be a very large but fallow field.

There was not light enough for Dex to be sure, but he thought the land had once been planted to cotton. Probably it had been "cottoned out" from years of use, he assumed, and would lie idle for a few years now as Carter tried to increase his yields from it.

Dex hadn't paid all that much attention to the farming back home—that was more in his greedy brother's line of interest—but he remembered that their father believed cotton land recovered better if occasionally planted to alfalfa or some other less lucrative crops. Charles Yancey had believed that the temporary reduction of income paid dividends in the long run. Dex considered mentioning that to Carter, then decided against it. Not only was it none of his damn business, it was the sort of advice that can create argument. And Dex did not want Grand Dragon Harry Carter or anyone else looking for excuses to oppose him. Not about anything whatsoever.

The Wharburton Klavern was assembled before the illustrious guest of honor arrived. There were, Dex estimated, a good sixty or seventy men gathered inside a ring of bonfires.

Every one of the men, he was both amused and pleased to see, was wearing a white hood now, not the individually decorated green that had been in vogue prior to Dex's instruction.

The plain hoods, he'd explained to the Wharburton officers, did not permit identification of any individual Klansman and were therefore all the more menacing to those who might need to be . . . admonished.

Admonished. That was the term Dex recalled General Forrest using.

He rather supposed that tonight it would be a Klan member who was admonished.

Dex hoped the son of a bitch got a whipping every bit as bad as the one he'd given James. It would serve the bastard right.

Without regalia—dammit, he realized, he should have thought to provide himself with a hood and staff and maybe some other fancy-looking shit—Dex marched boldly into the center of the mass of Klan members.

"I see you've delayed lighting the crosses until I arrived," Dex observed. "That was thoughtful of you, thanks."

At the front of the gathering ground three tall crosses had been erected, each constructed of what looked like kiln-dried lumber and each at least ten feet tall. At the base of each was a pile of scantlings, and Dex could smell coal oil, so presumably the crosses and kindling alike were well prepared to take flame at the touch of the ceremonial torch.

The burning cross lay at the heart of the Klan's convictions, Dex knew from his conversations with General Forrest. Often misunderstood by the uninformed, the cross was a symbol not of hate but of truth, not of evil but of justice. The cross was not consumed by the fire but illuminated by it so that all men could know that the precepts of Christianity were honored by the Klan in its ceremonies. And in its other activities, too. Just as the cross itself and all it stood for were dedicated to good, Forrest advocated, so must the Klan devote itself to the triumph of good over evil. The illuminated cross was symbolic of this devotion and a reminder to those who saw it that their actions would be judged. By the spiritual powers above. And by the temporal powers of the Ku Klux Klan below.

Grand Dragon Carter mounted a small platform set close in front of the three crosses, and immediately a hush fell over the babbling Klansmen as they saw and gave their attention.

"Brother Knights," Carter announced in a voice loud enough for all to hear. "You know the reason we are here. We are honored by a visit from the Imperial Wizard, Dexter Lee Yancey of Blackgum Bend Plantation, Louisiana."

Dex realized that he'd forgotten to inform the Grand Dragon that the title was properly Grand Imperial Wizard. Oh well. Another time, perhaps.

"Give the Imperial Wizard a Wharburton welcome, boys."

The crowd exploded into roaring shouts of acclamation. It was enough to flatter a boy, Dex thought. Damn near enough to make him want to join the Klan himself.

Carter motioned for the men to become quiet. After a few seconds the commotion died down, and Carter spoke again. "Brother Knights, I told you already that we are honored by this visit from the Imperial Wizard. Most of you already know, however, that we have been dishonored in his eyes by the conduct of certain of our members."

That statement elicited a growl of disapproval from beneath the hoods.

"We ain't like that, Harry," someone shouted.

"No man here would steal from the Order," another yelled.

"Three men here did indeed steal from the Order," Carter responded so quickly that Dex suspected the shouted comments had been scripted beforehand. "Three of those who claimed to be our brothers did steal. Their crime is not what they took from the Imperial Wizard's nigger. None of us knew at the time that the money belonged to the Klan. No, brothers, their crime is that these three took some of that money and put it into their own pockets. They knowingly stole from you. They stole from me. They stole from the Wharburton Klavern. They violated the trust they were given, and they tried to subvert our great and glorious Order for their own profit."

Carter swept his hood off and stood in the firelight glaring at the Klansmen before him as if accusing them, too. "Is that what we have become?" he shouted.

"No!" the roar came instantly back at him.

"Do we condone this behavior?"

"No!"

"If our right hand offends us, what must we do?"

"Cut it off!" The roar was slightly less vigorous this time. Dex suspected some of the clods out there behind the hoods didn't know the proper answer to that one.

"Sergeant at Arms," Carter shouted.

"Aye, sir." It was Garrison, of course. Dex thought he would have recognized the man from his size alone even if he hadn't already known that Barney Garrison filled that office.

"Bring the prisoners forward."

The crowd in the center of the meeting grounds parted, and six hooded Klansmen proceeded through them in pairs, each dragging a bound and gagged "brother" between them. The prisoners, Dex noted, were not wearing hoods, white or green. Instead what looked like their old green hoods had been wadded and stuffed into their mouths, tied in place there with strips of cloth.

The men were disheveled, their hair wildly disordered and their clothing torn and bloody. It was obvious that they had been beaten severely.

Good, Dex thought. Served the SOBs right for these would have been among the five who beat James nearly to death. The pricks.

"These foul creatures who claimed brotherhood have been interrogated," Carter shouted to his flock. "They have confessed their crimes. The money they stole from us was recovered. Now they face the wrath of true justice." The Grand Dragon took a deep breath. "What say you, Brother Knights?"

The volume of sound that ripped from the throats of the Klansmen was loud enough to put night birds into the air for two miles in any direction. The noise damn near caused the ground to tremble, Dex thought. Or anyway it made his knees shake. Which surely was caused by the ground quivering, right?

It occurred to Dex that he could be damn well grateful that it was these SOBs who were the object of such furor and not he.

"Sergeant at Arms," Carter yelled when the noise abated enough for him to be hear again.

"Aye, Your Excellence?"

"Sergeant at Arms, do your duty."

"Aye," Garrison shouted back. He motioned and his aides dragged the pale and wild-eyed three forward.

The men were hauled to the crosses, pressed tight against the rough-hewn uprights and lashed in place there with their backs to the wood and facing outward to the men who'd once called them brothers.

Dex had it figured out now, and damn clever, too. The men had already been beaten. Now they would be humiliated as an example before the others. Likely they would be beaten again or even lashed before they were finally ejected from the Klavern in disgrace.

Whoever these men were, Dex thought, they were finished in Wharburton. With this many of the townspeople set hard against them, each man among the three would be forever a pariah. They would be doing themselves and their families a favor, Dex realized, if they would pack up as soon as they were healed enough to travel. Pack up and leave Wharburton never to return.

For half an instant Dex felt a pang of sympathy for the men. They'd beaten James, yes. They deserved punishment. But even he thought that this measure was extreme. No man should suffer forever for a mistake as small as pilferage.

Dex was tempted to speak. To intercede. He thought about it. Then realized that would only lessen the respect he now enjoyed among these Loyal Knights of the Ku Klux Klan.

He did not want to risk that just to keep three cheating, thieving sons of bitches like these from taking a beating such as they'd given to James.

Dex kept his mouth shut and his arms folded.

"Sergeant at Arms," Carter shouted.

"Aye, sir."

"Do your duty."

The eyes of two of the men bulged practically out of their heads, and dark stains appeared at their crotches and spread swiftly down their trousers. The third man, the one on the right, passed out completely, sagging limp and senseless against the ropes that bound him to the base of the wooden cross.

Barney Garrison picked up what looked like a long, slender club with a dark lump at its head. Tar, Dex thought. Tar and feathers? But that did not make sense. Where was the other stuff? Where was the cauldron of hot tar or the bags of feathers? They didn't have the proper stuff here to tar and feather anyone.

Garrison walked to the nearest bonfire and shoved the end of the "club" into the flames.

Oh, Jesus! Dex thought wildly. Surely they wouldn't . . .

• 45 •

"I didn't . . . I swear to you, I didn't think they'd really do it," Dex said in a halting, gasping voice. "Even when I saw what he was doing, I thought they were only trying to put the fear into those men. I didn't think they would really . . . oh, Jesus!"

"Are you all right?" James asked.

Dex shrugged. "Sure, I'm . . . no, I guess I'm not. Not really. It was . . . awful, James. It was just awful."

"You don't have to talk about it if you don't want to."

"Talk about it? James, I can still *see* it. I can't hardly see or think about anything else. It just keeps happening in my mind, and I see it over and over and over again. The way the flames caught. The expressions on those poor sons of bitches. I mean . . . I hate what they did to you, James. But . . . what a terrible, awful, horrid way to die.

"The fire and the smoke. The look in their eyes. Tied up there. Couldn't even scream out. Couldn't get away. The flames . . . James, their hair burst into fire. Before the other fire got all the way up that high, their hair burst into flame. I didn't . . . I wouldn't have thought it would do anything like that. I hope . . . maybe they were dead by then. I couldn't tell. God, I hope they were dead.

"And their clothes. Their pants caught fire and flared up and then . . . then their hair . . . and finally everything in between.

"And the smell. That was the worst of it, I think. The smell. Burnt meat and the stink of burning hair. It smelled . . . God help me, but it smelled kind of like the smoke from a barbecue mixed in with the smell when a horse or a cow is branded and the hair is singed. It was . . . I can still smell it. I can smell it so strong the taste of it is in my mouth, James.

"On my way back here just now I had to stop alongside the road and puke. Threw up everything I've had to eat for the past three days, but the taste that's in my mouth right now is like the smell of those dead men burning up along with the crosses they were tied to. I never . . . I never thought—"

"It isn't your fault, Dexter. You didn't know, and you didn't cause it to happen."

"But what kind of people would do something like that, James? What kind of awful people are these?" It was a question to which Dex had no answer. "They aren't like any Klansmen I ever knew or heard about. God, you know how the Klan was back home. You know what the general intended for it to be. That's what I've always known it to be like. Decent and honorable. The whole idea of the Klan was for folks to have justice. Not just whites either. Everybody. Damn Reconstruction soldiers and carpetbag politicians were stealing land and lording it over decent people. Taking what they wanted and running the courts and the law, so anything they wanted to do was all right, and honest people couldn't get justice. The Klan put a stop to that. Night riders, sure. Vigilantes, sure. But always for the good. Always opposing evil. What they wanted, what they saw that people got, was justice. Hard justice sometimes, but it was always for the right. It was never anything like . . . this."

Dex shivered and wrapped his arms tight around his torso in a futile effort to rid himself of the chill that threatened to invade his soul. "James, these people don't stand against evil. These people *are* evil. Evil personified and walking on the earth. That isn't the Klan, James. That isn't the fine thing that General Forrest created."

"Maybe not," James said, "but it is what these people have made of what he did."

"It's an abomination is what it is," Dex said. He shuddered. "To do something like that . . . even if those men deserved to die . . . just to be able to do it like was done . . . it's beyond me, James. I simply don't understand how anyone could be like that.

"And I . . . God help me, James, I stood right there and acted just as awful and as evil as all of them were. I was scared. God, I was scared. If they found out the truth about you and me . . . I spoke to them. Even while the bodies were there charred and stinking, I made a speech to the rest of them. Damned if I know what I said. Some sort of bullshit, I suppose. I honestly don't know. I remember that I said something. Exhorted them. Jesus, maybe I praised them. I don't recall. They gave me the money belt." He glanced down at it lying beside him on the running board of the brougham. "I guess our money is all there. I didn't count it. I . . . I didn't really care. You know?"

"Of course you didn't," James said in a gentle, soothing voice. "You aren't like them, Dex. I want you to think about that for a minute. You aren't like those people. The general wasn't like those people. And the Klan, the real Ku Klux Klan, it isn't like those people either. You should try and remember that, Dexter."

"You know what I can't figure out, James?"

"What's that?"

"Why'd they go and *do* that to those men? They stole, sure. They were weak, yes. But . . . that?"

"You know what strikes me about what you've told me t'night?" James asked. "They brought these men out in front of you and the other Klansmen already beat up and bound and gagged."

"That's right. So?"

"Beat and bound, yeah, I can see why they might want to do that. But what makes me wonder, Dex, is why were they already gagged. What might those three men have had to say that the others didn't want said? And come to think of it, who are the others? There were five of them that beat me up and took our money belt. Three of those five were executed tonight. So who are the other two and why weren't they beat up and burned too?"

Dex gave James a bleak look, having barely heard his friend's questions. "I feel sick to my stomach. I want to go in and go to bed now. I think . . . I don't think anyone will bother you again. But keep your guns close to hand anyway, just in case."

"Go to bed, Dex. Go in and have a couple stiff drinks, then go up to bed. Try not to think about it."

Dex shuddered. "I'm telling you, I can still smell their hair burning and hear the fat in the one guy's body sizzle and pop. I can smell . . . oh, Jesus. Oh, Jesus God!" he blurted and ran for the doorway with a hand over his mouth, barely making it outside before he spewed hot stomach acids, all that was left in his belly to disgorge, onto the camellias planted in old Mr. Barr's elegant garden.

⋄ 46 ⋄

Dex was still feeling shaky and out of sorts in the morning. He'd slept poorly, and his stomach not only ached from emptiness, he was belching acids and foul flavors as well.

All in all he had not passed an especially pleasant night.

Unsure if he even wanted to eat anything, by the time he got downstairs and smelled the mingled aromas of the breakfast Mrs. Collum laid out his mouth was filling with saliva so fast he had to swallow repeatedly lest he drown himself in his own juices. The smells of ham and bacon, hot biscuits and cold fruits, flannel cakes and cane syrup made him suddenly as ravenous and eager as moments earlier he'd been skeptical of his own capacity to eat. Dex was barely able to contain himself long enough to greet Mr. Barr and wait while his elderly host mumbled a blessing over the meal. Then Dex dug in up to both elbows. Figuratively speaking, that is. He might have done it literally except he did not want to shock Mr. Barr.

"You are in good appetite this morning," the old gentleman observed.

"I'm sorry, sir. I don't mean to be rude."

Barr waved the apology away. "Don't be foolish. I was not complaining, I assure you. It is just that at my age I don't

have the desire for food that I once enjoyed. Nor other de-
sires either for that matter. No, son, it's good to see someone
enjoy himself for a change. Not much of that to be found in
this house nowadays, I fear."

"Yes, sir." Even so Dex forced himself to slow—but not
eliminate—the assault he was making on a mountain of fried
potatoes and a side dish of berries with cream. He'd already
wrapped himself around a pound of bacon and almost the
same amount of ham. Well, more or less. He wasn't actually
keeping track of the exact amounts, just knew that everything
tasted almighty good to him in the light of this new day.

When he finally declared himself full, Mr. Barr smiled
approval at this feat of record-setting consumption. "Would
you care for anything else, Dexter?" The old man sounded
half amused by the spectacle Dex had created while the other
half was in awed admiration.

"Thank you, sir, but I've had quite enough now."

"Shall we take our coffee onto the porch? I like to sit out
at this hour when everything is so cool and fresh and still."

"Yes, sir, I'd like that, but I think—"

"Mrs. Collum has already taken something out to your
man if that is what concerns you."

"Thank you, sir. It would be my pleasure to join you."
Mr. Barr asked little enough of Dex in return for his unques-
tioning hospitality. If the old gentleman would enjoy a little
company now, it would be more than a pleasure for Dex to
provide it.

Mr. Barr seemed frail this morning so Dex took both cups
and saucers and carried them outside. He arranged them on
a small wicker table situated between two ladderback rocking
chairs and waited for Mr. Barr to be seated before Dex lowered himself into the other rocker.

Mr. Barr was right. The air was particularly pleasant in
the early morning. There were the delicate scents of rose
blossoms and jasmine, and somewhere not too far away a
woman had taken bread fresh from the oven. Dex was not
sure which of the three scents he liked the best.

Any of them was in sharp and welcome contrast with his memories from the night before.

He still was having difficulty accepting the fact of what Harry Carter and his hooded thugs had done.

"Mr. Barr."

The old gentleman set his cup back onto the saucer with a rattle. "What is it, son?"

"What can you tell me about a neighbor of yours named Harry Carter?"

Barr's normally genial expression became hard. "How do you know that man, Dexter?"

"I met him the other evening. I take it from your response that you and he are not, shall we say, close?"

"Hardly," Barr said in a cold and uncompromising voice. "And that man is no neighbor of mine. We only live in the same town."

"I didn't mean to distress you, sir."

"Not your fault, of course. You didn't know."

"Would it bother you to tell me what you can about him?"

Barr harrumphed and fidgeted for a moment, wasted a little time fussing with his coffee cup and drinking from it. Dex guessed he was putting his thoughts in order.

"I try to be a fair man," Barr said at length.

"Yes, sir. That is one of the things my father most admired about you, Mr. Barr."

"Before I say anything else, Dexter, you should clearly understand that whatever I tell you will be tainted by prejudice."

"Sir?"

"I dislike Harold Carter. Always have. Always will. He is a cheat and a charlatan and no gentleman, I can tell you that much. That man is no gentleman."

To Edgar Barr, Dex knew, as to his own father Charles Yancey there was little worse that could be said about a man than that he was no gentleman. A man could be stingy or mean or abusive, he could break laws or be a knee-walking drunk. Those things could be forgiven. Being deemed without gentlemanly qualities, though, was worse than any or all of them.

"Harry is from Wharburton originally. Decent enough family. The Carters were among the original landholders under the Stephen Austin agreement with Mexico, you see. That means something here. But Harold's father Leonard hadn't a lick of sense. Went head over heels for a high yella girl. Would have married that little nigger girl if it hadn't been for the law getting in his way. Bold as brass about it, Leonard was.

"Stupid in other ways, too. Everything he'd inherited he gambled away or gave away to the girl and her endless string of relatives. Or niggers claiming to be relatives. Who knew the truth about that, of course. Poor Leonard never knew. Doubt he ever cared. The man became a laughingstock, and Harold with him. Couldn't last here in Wharburton as I'm sure you understand, so about the time Harold was . . . oh, I can't say for sure . . . fourteen, fifteen years old I suppose, they sold what little they still owned and left.

"News travels, of course. Leonard took the family down to the coast. Went out 'onto Galveston Island and tried his hand at business. He was no damned good at that either, or so we heard. He died . . . it would have been before the war some time. I'm not sure when.

"Harold was old enough to take charge by then, and like I told you he was no gentleman. I gather there wasn't much he wouldn't have been willing to take a profit from. His father gambled. Harold was no gambler. He wanted the sure thing. So he opened a gaming house. Not a gentleman's club, mind, but the sort of place frequented by sailors and drunks and other riffraff. I don't doubt that the games were fixed and the whiskey drugged. He had whores there. Cheap and bawdy women too eaten up with the pox to find work anywhere else. Harold would take them in, use them up, and then spit them out. Oh, we were a long way away, but we heard, Dexter. We heard all about it."

"Yes, sir."

"When the war came and the damned Yankees took over, Harold was in his glory. Decent Southerners shunned the bluebelly bastards. Harold welcomed them. As long as they had money to spend, they were welcome in his place. Places, I should say. Harold had money at a time when no one else in Texas did. He raked in all he could get, and he bought and sold and profited like a fat hog at a trough. Harold Carter came out of the war a rich man, and afterward his business interests and land holdings made him even richer. God knows what he was worth when he finally decided that he had enough money. What he wanted then was to buy respectability. And where he wanted to do it was right back here in Wharburton.

"That pusillanimous peckerwood Harold Carter decided to come home, damn him. He came back here, bought that big old mansion from some son of a bitch lawyer representing Jonas Dort's estate . . . never trust a lawyer, son, let this be a lesson to you."

"Yes, sir."

"Where was I? Oh, yes. Harold came home. Bought that big old house when no one else would sell to him and had it rebuilt. Damn thing was falling apart when he got it. He likes to give the impression now that it's the Carter family's ancestral manor house or some crap like that. Ha! Leonard Carter's place was torn down years ago to make room for a stable. Damn sight better use for it too, I say. I only wish someone would turn this new place into a pig sty. That would be more appropriate.

"Anyway, Harold has been trying ever since to make himself over into a respectable gentleman. Easier to turn dog shit into doughnuts. But he keeps trying. Tried to buy his way into politics, but no one would vote for him. Tried to buy up land so he could have a plantation of his own . . . to expand the brand new ancestral estate, I suppose . . . but no decent land owner around Wharburton would sell to him.

"And as far as I know he's still trying. The son of a bitch. And if you are wondering, Dexter, why I sound so damn-all bitter about this, I'll tell you. It's because eventually it will be Harold Carter who winds up owning my Windthistle Plantation, damn him. The Dort place only sits on a few acres, right on my north property line. I know good and well when my place goes up for sheriff's auction Harold Carter will be the one to bid it in. And that pisses me off, Dexter. It just naturally pisses me off.

"Son, tell me something. And be honest about it. Do you think it too early to pour a dollop of brandy into this coffee?"

Dex smiled and quickly stood. "I'll be right back with the brandy, sir."

"Thank you, Dexter. Now you and your daddy, you are gentlemen. Thank you."

"Yes, sir." Dex hurried back inside the house to fetch out the decanter of French brandy and a bit of sugar to go along with it.

· 47 ·

Dex could not get the past night out of his mind. Nor could he forget Edgar Barr's conversation after breakfast. Harold Carter was at the heart of both events, damn him.

After checking to make sure James was all right Dex took James' breakfast tray back to Mrs. Collum inside the house, then secured his coat, hat and cane and went for a stroll in the woods. Well, sort of.

He followed the public road south past Harry Carter's non-ancestral mansion and beyond. When the road curved away from the river, Dex began looking for a path or farm road. He knew there had to be one. He came to a pair of ruts that showed little sign of recent use and turned off the main road there, ambling along as if he hadn't a care in the world with nothing furtive or sneaking about his presence. If anyone were to observe or inquire—unlikely, but who could know— he would arouse no suspicion.

The farm road passed by a tiny plot of cleared ground that would once have been planted to a vegetable garden, briefly re-entered the thicket and opened once again onto a clutch of four cabins built at the edge of a field of sixty or perhaps seventy acres' extent.

The cabins would once have been slave quarters, Dex was sure, and later the homes of hired men or sharecroppers.

They were in poor repair now, and the one furthest east showed the charring of fire.

This would be Mr. Barr's land, Dex guessed, and these the houses that once were occupied by his people. People who'd been run off by the Wharburton Klavern of the KKK.

It was interesting, Dex thought, that Harry Carter hungered for land. That Edgar Barr owned land adjacent to Carter's home but would not sell to him. That Harry Carter was Grand Dragon of the Klan hereabouts. And that Mr. Barr's ability to earn a living had been destroyed when the KKK decided to evict all persons of color from this vicinity.

All of it entirely a matter of unrelated coincidence, Dex assured himself as he mulled the collage of facts.

He peered into the gaping windows and doorless doorframes of each of the cabins, finding nothing inside, but was reluctant to take the next logical step in his daylight examinations.

Finally, unable to fool himself any longer, he took a deep breath and walked down to the far east end of the fallow cotton field.

The stubble of the last crop to grow here had been trampled flat on the broad area where Carter brought his Klansmen for their meetings.

Circles of dark ash showed where the crosses had been, and the embers of the ring of bonfires still smoldered and stank.

There was no sign this morning of the crosses themselves, Dex saw. Nor was there any hint that three men had died here last night.

Three last night, he thought. How many before that? People had disappeared from the county before. How many ran away? How many ended here instead? What passed for law in this end of the county was a participant in the slayings. Last night Deputy Barney Garrison himself applied the torch to the killing pyres. How many others might there have been before those unfortunate three?

Dex stood for a long time. Thinking. Trying to draw fact and assumption together into a cohesive whole in his mind.

At length he walked through the fringe of trees to reach the banks of the dark, slow-flowing Trinity. It was peaceful there, and a breeze carried the smell of ash and death away from him.

He leaned against the trunk of an ancient tree and silently watched the moving water, losing track of time completely. He did not budge again until a rumbling in his stomach informed him that he was hungry and, reawakening to the world about him, he realized that while he pondered the sun had passed its zenith and the afternoon was well advanced.

Dex's fingers lightly stroked the grip of the .455 Webley that rode at his waist, and he was conscious of the hard bulk of its mate tucked out of sight in the small of his back.

The sensible thing, he knew good and well, would be for him to go back to Mr. Barr's house and thank the old gentleman for his help and his hospitality. Hire—buy if he had to—a well-sprung light wagon and load James into it. James was fit enough to travel that way by now. And they wouldn't have to go far each day.

Aye, that would be the sensible thing. Leave Wharburton. Travel along slow and easy. Put this town and its problems behind them.

There was nothing to keep them here. They had their money back.

There was no reason at all they should stay.

Dex cleared his throat. Spat.

No reason to stay whatsoever.

They would leave.

Bright and early tomorrow if he could find a suitable wagon this afternoon.

They could be gone by the time the sun lifted above the forest treetops.

Dex scowled.

Bullshit, they would leave tomorrow. No fucking way.

Feeling considerably better—admittedly foolish perhaps, but a damn sight better—Dex squared his shoulders and headed back in the direction of town.

· 48 ·

"Inflation is hell," Dex grumbled.

"What's that?"

"Inflation. It means—"

"I know what it means, asshole. What I'm wondering is what the hell brought that up," James retorted.

"I needed a note delivered this afternoon, so I got a boy to carry it for me. A white boy, of course, since there isn't the usual flock of burr-headed picaninnies in this town. It cost me a dime. A niggerbaby would've only cost me a nickel."

"The boy demanded a dime from you just to carry a note to somebody?"

"No, he didn't demand anything. But I gave him a dime. I'd have given a nickel if he'd been black."

"So why'd you give the white boy a dime instead of the nickel the job was worth?"

"Just . . . because, that's all. But it pisses me off that it cost me a dime instead of the nickel. You see what I mean? Inflation. Run all the blacks off, and the next thing you know you have inflation. It's ugly, I tell you. Ugly."

"Sometimes, Dex, I think you're crazy as hell. You know that? Even for a white man, you're one crazy son of a bitch sometimes. Now are you gonna tell me or aren't you?"

"Tell you what?" Dex asked.

"Look, I know you pretty well by now. You stand there grumbling and mumbling like you're some kind of racist white trash, and I know better than that. But you brought all this shit up for a reason. And I know what that is, too. You want me to ask you about the note. So all right. I'm asking. What was in it and who'd you send it to?"

Dex grinned. "I am a genius. You know that, don't you?"

"What I know is that you are one crazy son of a bitch of a white boy. There's only one genius between the two of us, and you ain't him. Now are you gonna tell me or aren't you?"

Dex told him. Briefly. And then, sobering, said, "What I want you to know, James, is that this thing could work out . . . let's say it could happen in a manner other than what I want. And after I'd already sent the damn note I got to thinking about that. It isn't too late for me to postpone things. I could move you out of here first. Get you off to a safe distance and leave the money with you. That way if . . . like if I didn't come back to join you again or something . . . you'd have something to go on with when you get well enough to travel on your own again."

"Like hell I'd do that. But you're right about one thing. It isn't too late to forget this. You could call it off. Send another note. Get the hell out of here."

Dex shook his head. "You know I won't do that."

"Then postpone it. At the very least postpone it a little while. Just a few days should be enough. Let me get back on my feet so I can come with you. It'd be better for you if there was somebody there to watch your back, Dex. Otherwise—"

Dex laughed. "You dumb black bastard. Doesn't that sound like just one helluva idea. You. At a KKK meeting. Doesn't that sound just dandy-keen."

"Don't be so quick to say no, dammit. I could wear a hood. Gloves, too. None of those offay cocksuckers would have to know. I could be right there behind you, boy."

Dex smiled and shook his head. "And to think. A minute ago *you* were calling *me* crazy."

"Hey. I mean it, you know."

"Shit, James, I know you do. You'd stand there and throw buckets of water into Hell, too, if you thought it would help me. But I can't let you do it. Apart from all the other obvious reasons against it, if anything goes wrong I have no intention of trying to shoot it out with sixty or seventy wild-ass Klansmen. What I'm gonna do, James, is wear dark clothes and be prepared to run like hell. Now. D'you want me to take you on to the next town or do you think you can make it out of here on your own if, you know, if for some reason I can't come back here after?"

"I guess I'll take my chances here," James said. "But let me tell you something, buster. If you go and get your lily white ass killed, I won't *never* forgive you."

"I will keep that firmly in mind," Dex said in a bone-dry voice.

· 49 ·

"How do I look?" Dex asked, flicking imaginary specks of lint from his lapels and turning this way and that for James' inspection.

"You'll knock 'em dead."

"Careful what you say there. It could come to that."

"Yes, and if it does then better them than you. Just remember one thing."

"Mm?"

"If there's trouble, first you duck. Then you run like hell."

"Count on it." Dex was wearing a black suit and what he and James both thought was a thoroughly wicked-looking black hood. Unlike the baggy, saggy, flour sack sort of white hoods the rank and file Klansmen here in Wharburton had lately adopted, Dex had chosen to make his stand up in a tall peak that added nearly a full foot to his apparent height. The back of the hood flowed down over his back—all the better to keep him hidden in the dark if he had to bolt—but the front was cut away to expose most of his face, this on the theory that if there was trouble it might be a nice idea to be able to see what was coming at him.

"I think I'm ready." He picked up the cane, very much aware of the slim steel sword blade concealed within the malacca shaft. His hope was that he would not have to use the sword or the Webleys.

But if it did come to that, it was just as James said: Better them than him, damn them.

"Don't be late," James said. "I might want you to fetch me a snack in the middle of the night or something. You know?"

Dex took a long, last look at his friend lying on his pallet in the corner of the carriage house. Neither of them said anything more. Then Dex turned and strode purposefully out into the night.

Dex arrived at the field roughly half an hour past the time he had specified the Klan was to gather. He came by way of the road and farm path, past the old slave quarters. From there he crossed the fallow cotton field and made his way along the edge of the clearing so he could appear without warning from an unexpected direction, a bit of dramatic flourish never being amiss if you want to befuddle or dominate the other fellow.

The Klansmen were there, all right. Perhaps even more of them tonight than there had been for the executions. The bonfires had been renewed and blazed high, bright-burning embers rising into the cool air like so many thousands of suicidal fireflies climbing to their end.

It occurred to Dexter that with thoughts like that in mind he was being rather morbid.

But then this place, and these people, did tend to have that effect, he conceded.

Dex paused for a moment behind one of the bonfires, still out of sight of the Klansmen. He took a deep breath, then walked swiftly into the crowd and, head high, marched through them to the platform where Grand Dragon Harry Carter was holding forth.

"Quiet!" Dex bellowed as the Knights parted before him. "Silence. All of you. There is a great wrong to be set right tonight. Be quiet and hear the truth."

Dex leaped onto the platform and shouldered Carter to the side. He stood before the Knights with his feet spread wide and his hands on his hips. He suspected—hoped—that the peaked hood made him look ten feet tall, and the firelight playing over his somber clothing should give him an appearance of mystery and total power.

Lordy, he sincerely hoped that was the impression he gave off. He needed all the help he could get.

He glowered out across the crowd of men in white hoods who stood before him, not speaking again for a moment. He looked them over slowly, finding and staring directly into the empty eye sockets of the hoods as if he were peering into the souls of the men within them. He took his time about it, making a mental note of where Barney Garrison was standing. The big Sergeant at Arms could be recognized by his size regardless of the hood that hid his identity in theory only.

Finally Dex spoke, his voice loud and hard.

"There is evil work that has been done in this place," he said. "The sanctity of the Loyal Knights of the Ku Klux Klan has been violated. I want you to know that I had the honor, the privilege, to be personally acquainted with General Nathan B. Forrest. I learned from his own lips the majesty and the purpose of this glorious Order.

"You Knights of the Wharburton Klavern have been used for purposes that demean the integrity of the Order. You have been used for base purpose. For personal gain and for a coward's glory," Dex declared in a loud, firm voice that rang across the clearing.

"Your own Grand Dragon has violated his sacred oath and used the Knights of the glorious Klan to advance his own interests. You! Hold!" Dex roared, holding a hand palm outward as Garrison started forward.

"He's lying," Carter was shouting unheeded at the side of the platform. "Don't listen to him, men. This man is lying. He—"

"The men who died here last night were innocent," Dex continued. "The true thieves were your so-called Grand Dragon and your spurious Sergeant at Arms. That is why those men wore gags when they were brought before you. The true perpetrators could not allow the cries of the innocent to be heard." Actually Dex didn't have the least idea if that were accurate or not. But it sounded good, and it could have been true. And another charge to toss into the mix couldn't do any harm.

He turned toward Carter and thrust his left hand out, accusing forefinger extended. "Surrender yourself to the Knights of the Order and stand to judgment you foul and loathsome creature. I declare you excommunicated from the company of these and all true and honorable Knights. In the name of the Klan, in the name of all that is true and holy, I rebuke you, Harold Carter." Dex spun, the finger turning with his body and pointing unerringly at Barney Garrison. "I rebuke you as well." It would have sounded more impressive had he known for sure what Barney's proper first name was, but a guy can't have everything, can he.

"Knights of the Ku Klux Klan," he ordered, "take these men into custody."

The hooded men standing closest to Garrison, thank goodness, grabbed him in unthinking response to this voice of highest authority.

Unfortunately there was no one standing close to Harry Carter. No one, that is, but the Imperial Wizard himself.

· 50 ·

Harry Carter wanted his Klan back. At the very least he wanted Dexter Yancey silenced so Carter could soothe the feathers Dex went and ruffled. And toward that end, Grand Dragon Carter apparently decided that a little mayhem would be a nice idea.

With a roar of outrage—probably intensified by a large dose of fear in the event Dex's charges were accepted by the Knights—Harry Carter launched himself at the immensely tall figure in black who stood on the platform beside him.

Dex rapped him on the noggin with his cane. Sharply. The blow undoubtedly stung but could have caused no real physical damage. What it did do was to knock Carter's hood awry, twisting it about so that the eye holes were somewhere in the vicinity of the man's left ear and effectively blinding him.

Carter roared again, the sound of it slightly muffled by his hood.

Carter lost his footing, fell, snatched off his hood and tried to regain his feet. He became entangled in his own robes and fell again. Thrashing and cursing, the illustrious Grand Dragon ripped his robe off and threw it at Dexter.

The wad of satin cloth—Carter accepted nothing but the best for himself—struck Dex just above knee level and plopped harmlessly to the ground.

With a grin and a nod to the watching Knights, Dex unsheathed the sword from his cane and used the sharp tip of it to pierce the white satin robe and lift it high for all to observe.

Then with a wink and a shrug he tossed the robe casually aside and gave an awkwardly sprawled and quite thoroughly disheveled Harry Carter a sad shake of the head.

The Klansmen began to laugh at the sight of their glorious leader wallowing about on the wooden platform while Dex stood there unperturbed, his clothing not so much as rumpled.

It was the laughter that sent Carter over the edge of reason, Dex thought afterward. That or the knowledge that his activities could not withstand the scrutiny of the Klan.

And of course Harry Carter really did believe along with all the others that Dex was genuinely and truly the Grand Imperial Wizard of the Ku Klux Klan mother body.

Whatever the reasons, Harry Carter lost judgment, lost control, lost all sense and reason.

He also lost something rather more valuable than any of those or all of them. He lost his life.

Carter wobbled onto his knees, crouched for a moment and with a shriek of fury threw himself at Dexter, aiming more or less in the direction of Dex's nuts if only because that was the closest and most convenient target before him.

Dex did not consciously take time to think. He reacted. And since he had the sword already and rather unfortunately in hand it was Harry Carter's ill fortune to impale himself.

Carter's lunge carried him onto the point of Dex's sword, the blade entering at throat level, angle and impetus combining to send the steel sinking deep into his chest cavity.

Harry Carter dropped to his knees. He looked upward, his eyes meeting Dex's. For a long, anguished moment the two remained like that, eyes locked and figures as motionless as participants in a poetry society tableau. Harry Carter looked, Dex thought, quite puzzled by this entire turn of events. He blinked and his mouth opened as if he wanted to say something or perhaps to ask a question. His expression showed neither pain nor remorse but seemed instead to be plaintive and uncertain.

Then a trickle of blood appeared at the corner of Carter's mouth and dribbled onto his chin.

The light of life and reason ebbed from eyes that were suddenly dull, and a moment later Carter collapsed, the weight of his fall dragging the sword from Dex's hand.

Harold Carter had just left Wharburton again. This time he wouldn't be back.

Dex shook his head. He was not particularly sorry about Carter. But this wasn't exactly what Dex had wanted here tonight. There should have been a better way. There should have been—

"Look out!" someone in the crowd shouted.

· 51 ·

The men who'd been holding Barney Garrison captive apparently got so caught up in the sight of their Grand Dragon making first a spectacle and then a corpse of himself that they forgot just one little thing: to keep holding onto Barney Garrison.

Garrison obviously knew that there would be no way now to mollify or deny. The Knights at this point surely knew that the Grand Imperial Wizard's accusations struck home. Carter could not have acted as he did otherwise. And Garrison just as obviously did not want to end up like Carter, spitted on steel like a chicken on a skewer.

The powerful Sergeant at Arms—well, very recently former one anyway—jerked away from the inattentive hands that so lightly held him and jumped onto the platform.

Garrison was not leaping to the aid of his defunct partner in crime, though. Not hardly. He ignored Carter and before Dex realized what he was about grabbed the butt of the Webley that rode on Dexter's belt.

Garrison pressed the muzzle of the large caliber weapon hard against Dex's forehead and shouted, "Don't anybody move or try an' follow us. I'll shoot this son of a bitch, so help me I will. All I want, boys, is a head start, so don't nobody move and nothing more is gonna happen."

Dex swallowed. That was not, he discovered, very easy to do. In order to swallow he first had to get past the fist-sized lump that had lately developed in his throat.

Not that he really *needed* to swallow anyway, he quickly decided. He had no spit left in his mouth to worry about.

"Come along peaceful and quiet," Garrison growled.

"Real peaceful. Real quiet," Dex agreed, rather surprised that he could still speak. Never mind that the words came out in something of a squeak. He did get them out. That was much better than he'd expected.

Garrison turned his attention back to the Klansmen. "Nobody moves," he reminded them loudly. "Give me till all the fires die down. Nobody move till then or your fucking Wizard dies."

Bullshit, Dex thought. If Garrison got the head start he wanted, Dex was as good as a dead man already.

Not that Dex mentioned this aloud. He wasn't entirely sure he could have if he wanted to. At the moment all his concentration was focused on stopping a sudden urge to piss.

"You. That way." Garrison backed up half a pace and pointed with the barrel of the gun, off in the direction of the opening between bonfires where last night the three fatal crosses had been. That was the way toward the riverbank path Carter had led Dex along the first time he came here. It led eventually to the Carter mansion. To town. To freedom for those still alive to enjoy it.

Dex meekly stepped off the platform and headed in the direction Garrison wanted.

· 52 ·

"Stop here," Garrison ordered.

Dex stopped. They were on the brick footpath that led along the side of Harry Carter's house. The spot where Garrison wanted Dex to stand lay in a puddle of yellow lamplight that was shining out of a side window in the house. The area around them was in darkness, but here the light was good. Too damned good, Dex thought.

"Turn."

"Which way?"

"Face me."

"I'll give you credit for one thing, Garrison. You aren't afraid to look a man in the eye when you kill him."

"You think I'm going to kill you?"

"Of course you are."

"You came along like a little man, didn't you?"

"I was hoping for . . ." He shrugged. "Something. I don't know. In the woods, maybe. Thought you might fall down or I could get far enough ahead to duck and hide."

"I'm too smart for that."

Dex grunted. The son of a bitch intended to kill him and now he wanted compliments too? Fuck that!

"Could I ask a favor?"

"Shit, get down on your knees and beg if you want to. You can't run fast enough to get away from a bullet out of this here gun."

Dex noticed that at some point during their little walk through the woods Garrison had shoved Dex's lumpy Webley into his waistband and taken out his own pistol. Likely felt more comfortable with a gun he was used to. Not that it would have made any difference. Either one of them was plenty big enough to ruin a fellow's whole day if he was shot with it.

"I'll not give you the satisfaction of begging, Garrison, but if I have to meet my end I intend to do it like a gentleman should."

"How's that, Yancey?"

"With my head held high and looking back at you eye to eye, that's how."

"You think I can't shoot a man who knows it's coming?"

"That isn't the point. I'll not beg and I'll not grovel. May I have a moment to tuck myself in and tidy up a bit?"

Garrison snorted. But he didn't shoot.

"Thank you," Dex said stiffly.

He removed the tall, peaked black hood, folded it and dropped it onto the ground beside his right foot. He felt of his starched collar to make sure the points were lying flat and tugged once at his tie to assure himself it was correctly in place. He checked his sleeve cuffs, pulled at the front of his vest and reached around beneath the tail of his coat as if to tuck his shirt tail in back there.

Garrison was half bored with the whole thing by then.

Which Dex was quite counting on.

As a consequence Garrison did not notice until much too late that when Dexter's hand came back in view from the small of his back, that hand was no longer empty.

The twin Webley filled it.

Dex's first slug took Barney Garrison by surprise.

It also took him squarely between the eyes, creating a dark red indentation there but making something of a mess of the back of the big deputy's head.

Dex shuddered in disgust at the ugly sight, then stepped forward to retrieve the other Webley from Garrison's waistband.

· 53 ·

"Shouldn't we get the hell out of here?" James suggested. "Like right damn now before the sheriff comes?"

"I don't think the sheriff will be coming," Dex said. "There's been too many people killed and missing and too many so-called good citizens involved in all of it for anybody to want any sort of official investigation. If any one person was to come to trial, everybody likely would be dragged into it before it was all said and done. No, I think this town is willing to shut up and forget any of this ever happened.

"I talked about it with Mr. Barr this morning, and he's of the same opinion," Dex said.

"Will this make a difference to him?" James asked.

Dex sighed and shrugged. "There aren't any guarantees. The good thing is that he still has his land. And now it will be safe for people . . . field hands and like that . . . to come back to Wharburton. They won't be killed or beaten or run out of their homes just so Harry Carter can become a high-stepping plantation owner. We can be sure of that much. As for the rest, I really don't know. Mr. Barr won't have cash enough to hire employees, but he thinks he can get a banker friend over in Shreveport to go seed money for him. He can put the land out on shares. With luck, if the weather's good and the sharecroppers know what they're about ... just maybe it will work. I wouldn't expect things to ever be as fine and easy as they were in the past, but I suppose you can't have everything."

"God knows you try, though," James said with a smile.

Dex grinned back at him. "The good thing about it being safe for the field hands to come back," he said, "is that they'll bring their daughters with them. There will be some black girls around for you to spark about the time you get healed enough to have at one of them."

"God, I'd hope so. If it gets any worse I can start using this thing to hammer nails with. I never been so horny in my life, Dex."

"I suppose I could ride around the county and see can I find some dusky little thang to snuggle up to you, though I'd hate having to think of myself as a pimp from then on."

"Not only a pimp but pimping for a colored clientele," James said with obvious pleasure. "Y'know, I kind of like the sound of that. I—"

Whatever he intended to say was lost in a scream of "*You son of a bitch!*"

Startled, Dex looked up from his seat on the brougham running board to see a familiar but entirely unexpected figure in the doorway of the carriage house.

He had to search his memory for a moment to remember the name although the tits were familiar.

"Jane," he said.

"You bastard!"

"I don't understand," Dex said. It was an entirely true and correct statement. "Have I done something to ... offend you?"

Jane's normally pretty face was flushed a bright and mottled red, made splotchy and ugly with the patches of discoloration. She really did have great tits though. Not that Dex was paying much attention to them at the moment, however. Not after he caught sight of the shiny little object she had in her dainty hand.

The shiny device was a small, nickel-plated handgun. A muff gun, he believed was the proper term. It consisted of a palm-shaped grip, a revolving cylinder, and a trigger mechanism that looked like a ring. Except this ring was not decorative but deadly. There was virtually no barrel sticking out of the front of the ugly little gadget and Dex doubted that it would be accurate at anything more than a pace or two.

He stood up and moved backward a pace or two.

"Jane, honey, I don't understand. What have I—"

"You *bastard*," she hissed. "You murdered my father and now you don't know why I would be *mad* at you?"

"I mur . . . your father was Barney Garrison?" he sputtered.

Jane gave him what would have been a most withering look. If that is, Dex hadn't already been pretty well withered. "My father, you snake in the grass, was Harold Boyd Carter. The Carters are descended from the founding fathers of this country *and* from the first families of Texas."

There was a distinct possibility that Dex and Jane Carter were related, albeit at quite a distance. After all, Dex was kin to the Virginia Lees on his mother's side, and the Virginia Carter's were certainly kin to Lighthorse Harry Lee and even that exceptional gentleman Marse Robert himself.

He did not, however, think this an appropriate time to bring up familial genealogies.

"Jane, I think—"

"I am going to kill you, you bastard. First I am going to shoot your balls off. Then I am going to kill you."

Dex took another step backward.

Jane waved the ugly little gun rather alarmingly, gesturing with each word.

Dex wondered how many cartridges the muff gun held. And how many times he could count on Jane missing him if she started shooting.

"Count on" of course was the operative phrase there. He did not like the thought of having to "count on" the lady's marksmanship failing her. Or him.

"Don't try to get away. Stand still," she demanded.

Fat chance, Dex thought. He stepped quickly to the side.

Jane yanked the ring attached to the tiny gun. There was a crack like a brittle twig snapping, and Dex heard the world's largest bumblebee zip much too closely past his left ear.

She'd been aiming for his balls—or so she claimed she would—and damn near hit him in the head.

Somehow he did not think that an encouraging possibility.

"Dammit, Jane, I—"

The twig snapped a second time. This time Dex had no idea where the bullet went. He was busy trying to put the body of the brougham between Jane and himself.

Funny but he had no fond memories of her in connection with that brougham now, never mind what they'd done there before.

"Dammit, Jane—"

He heard the gun fire a third time, although at that point he was behind the brougham and completely out of her line of sight.

He waited for a moment, but there was no more shooting and no more shouting.

Carefully, ready to jump back at the snap of a trigger, Dex peered out from behind the carriage.

Jane was sprawled rather untidily on the floor. James was standing over her. He had one of his pistols in his hand, but he hadn't shot her with it. He held it reversed in his hand and quite obviously had whacked her on the head with the butt of his revolver.

"I didn't know you could stand up by yourself yet," Dex said.

"Neither did I," James told him.

"We were both wrong. Not that I'm complaining."

Jane began to move.

"I suppose we either have to hit her again or shoot her or maybe tie her up," James suggested. "What do you think?"

Dex sighed. "People might object if we kill her."

"There's some light straps over there," James said, pointing. "You could tie her up with that."

Dex grunted. And went to get the straps.

"You aren't well enough to travel," Dex said.

"I'm well enough to hang though. I don't see that as an improvement. Besides, we didn't think I was well enough to stand up on my own hind legs until just a little while ago."

"Why don't you see if you can't manage to do a little traveling," Dex suggested.

"Good idea." James looked down at Jane, who was trussed as neatly as a turkey on its way into a roaster. "What about her?"

"The choices haven't much changed. I still don't want to kill her."

"You gonna leave her like that?"

"Somebody will find her. Eventually. It will give us time to put Wharburton behind us," Dex said.

"You son of a bitch," Jane snarled. "You can run, but you won't get away from me. Do you hear me, you bastard? I'm a rich woman. I'll find you. Wherever you go, I'll find you. I'll hire men to hunt you down and shoot you like the dog you are, you miserable bastard. And your nigger, too." She glared at James. "You *hit* me, you black ape."

"Yes, ma'am," James said, although he did not sound especially contrite about it. "I did do that."

"And you, you, you—" She was sputtering and steaming to the point that she could no longer get words to flow coherently out of her mouth.

"If you leave her like that she's gonna holler and be found pretty quick," James said.

"I'm afraid you're right." He leaned down to Jane's level and said, "I don't take any pleasure from this. I want you to know that."

"I will have you hunted down and shot. Wherever you go, I will find you," she blustered. "I will spend every last cent of my papa's fortune to find you and have you killed. I will post a bounty on your head that a priest would kill for. I will—"

James handed him a rag—it was a smelly thing so filthy it was no longer possible to determine what its purpose or even its color might once have been—and Dex stuffed the cloth into Jane's mouth, stopping the flow of vituperation in mid-sentence.

"Better wrap this strip of cloth around too so she can't spit it out."

Dex improved upon the arrangement until both of them were satisfied that Jane could neither move on her own nor shout for help.

"I surely do feel up to doing some traveling today," James said as he looked down at a squirming, wiggling, and still furious Miss Carter.

Later, when they were some miles down the road, James asked Dex, "Tell me. Do you think that woman meant all that shit about hiring gunmen to come after us?"

Dex gave his friend a long, slow look. But he didn't say a word. He really didn't have to.